raph by Ron Jones

Brian Burland was born in Bermuda in 1931, largely of seafaring and clerical stock (and a few pirates and rum merchants), and educated at what he calls a "second rate" public school in England and several "mediocre" universities in Canada and the U.S.A. He worked at various jobs in Bermuda, the West Indies and New York ("selling toilets, stevedoring, going to sea and posing as a professor") and now lives in London. This is his first novel. It will certainly not be his last.

A FALL FROM ALOFT

This novel is exciting on three levels. First it is the adventure of a thirteen-year-old boy (of a hitherto sheltered upbringing) who suddenly finds himself serving as a boy on the lower decks on a freighter crossing the U-boat-infested waters of the Atlantic during the bitter winter of 1942; second it is the story of an unloved child tormented more by guilt over his perverse prepubescent sexuality and the desperate measures he has been forced to use to try to gain the attention from his parents than by the submarines, the sinkings and the pitiless sea itself; third it is a moving portrayal of the indefatigable courage and the ever-buoyant humour of seamen forced to endure abject terror seemingly past human capability.

But principally it is the story of a boy—and perhaps never before have a boy's mind, consciousness and reality been probed so deeply, exposed so nakedly, so honestly and so totally without sentimentality.

It is a study that may appal some readers but most will, if they are honest, recognise a part of themselves in this tormented child. *This is the way childhood was* and once one can accept it the story becomes human comedy and we experience what Hesse called that "laughter at the heart of things".

BRIAN BURLAND

A Fall from Aloft

BARRIE AND ROCKLIFF
THE CRESSET PRESS
LONDON

© BRIAN BURLAND 1968

FIRST PUBLISHED 1968 BY
BARRIE & ROCKLIFF, THE CRESSET PRESS
(BARRIE BOOKS LTD)
2 CLEMENT'S INN LONDON WC2

SET IN 10 PT TIMES

PRINTED IN GREAT BRITAIN BY
WESTERN PRINTING SERVICES LTD, BRISTOL

SBN 214.66722.7

FOR EDWINA ANN, MY LOVE,
AND A LOT OF FRIENDS—
MOST OF WHOM SEEM
TO BE NAMED JOHN

On a tombstone in the Royal Naval
Cemetery at Ireland Island, Bermuda
are written these words:

SACRED

TO THE MEMORY OF

MIDSHIPMAN JAMES CUMBERLAND

H.M.S. "IMMORTALITÉ"

KILLED BY A FALL FROM ALOFT

MAY 23rd 1777

AGED 13 YEARS

2 MOS

THIS TABLET WAS ERECTED BY

HIS SHIPMATES

Late in 1941 Hitler finally approved Admiral Doenitz's plan for a massive U-boat assault on Allied shipping throughout the Atlantic. By January 1942 the German Navy was able to maintain 130 U-boats operational in these waters at all times. In the months following the figure rose steadily.

Against them were the Royal Navy, the United States Navy and the Royal Canadian Navy. However, the Royal Navy, already stretched thin, had recently been forced to despatch large numbers of warships to the Far East; the United States Navy, ill-prepared, only very recently at war, disastrously threatened in the Pacific, was in a position where it was forced to ask the British to return some of the 50 destroyers loaned them earlier; the Royal Canadian Navy was suffering growing pains and had what the German High Command described as a penchant for sinking themselves.

Between the 1st of January and the 31st of July 1942 German U-boats sank, in the Atlantic alone, 3,000,000 tons of Allied shipping—a total of 568 merchant ships. In reply the Allies sank two U-boats in March and by July the grand total throughout the Atlantic and Arctic oceans was fourteen.

On the 3rd of February 1942, at the British Admiralty in London, a small convoy was pinned up on the map. Port of departure: Bermuda. Code name: B.H.X.167. Destination: United Kingdom via rendezvous 41° N, 43° W with a larger convoy shortly to sail from Halifax.

All plans were subject to sudden change for this was the time that Winston Churchill later described as The U-Boat Paradise...

A FALL FROM ALOFT

Homesickness. In certain nightmares caused by anxiety, people dream that they are falling; as they fall they experience a physical pain, a desperate hollowness of the lower abdomen. To be homesick is to endure this sensation continuously.

I

"Cor," someone below said, "the bleeder's movin'. Fuck, I didn't never want to leave this Bermuda place—lovely it is."

James lay in his bunk, his eyes open staring at the weld-scarred bulkhead above him. Although the ship was on her maiden voyage, rust was already showing through the thin grey paint.

"Leave it. Christ, I wish we'd never come near it. 'Aven't you heard? It was off Bermuda that the first one bought it. All 'ands too. Not one poor perisher saved. Christ I 'ate a ship with a dead ship's name."

"But the first *Empire United* wasn't torpedoed?"

"No, no, sprog—she was shat on by a virgin shyte-'awk."

"Cripes, I bet Hitler's submarines are right outside waitin' for us—let's go on deck, china."

"Pipe down, I'm 'aving a read."

About two feet from James's head was a large alarm bell. GENERAL ELECTRIC U.S.A. U.S.A. sometimes stood for United States Army, James thought, and if it was General Electric U.S. Army, we'd be on dry land. Dry land was what he'd longed for most, he thought, since he came on board the day before. Trees and soil and grass. He wished he was thirteen instead of just claiming to be thirteen, the way he always was, when he wouldn't really be thirteen for two

1

months. No, he thought, they could be at sea in the U.S. Army if this was a troopship.

"The Yanks built her as a landing barge carrier," James had heard an officer say, "that's why she's got this flat bottom —then they had too many of those so they stuck another deck on and called her a troopship. Then they tear all the bunks out of her, call her a freighter and give her to us. Ruddy thing would capsize on a trip around Brighton pier."

The propeller shaft, which ran directly under their quarters, gave a shudder and then made a sound that managed to be both shrill and thunderous at the same time.

Shra-a-gronk-orank.

Silence.

"If I've gotta hear that racket all the way to Blighty I'll go balmy."

"Bleeding Yanks. 'Oo ever 'eard of a fo'c'sle in the arse-end of a ship."

"You-can-say-that-again, mate. All the way across the Atlantic shoved up the arse of a fuckin' great tin whale."

James felt as if he was going to throw up. He'd felt seasick ever since he came on board although this motion, as the ship rode up on her anchor, was the first she had made.

Kling-kling.

James looked at the new wristwatch his father had given him. Five o'clock. Why two rings if it's five o'clock? Then, at the thought of his father—so close still but soon, he knew, to be irrevocably far away, gone, lost—his stomach gave a heave downwards feeling empty yet heavy, as if he'd swallowed buckshot like Mark Twain's frog, he thought. Home, warm fires and Grampy's voice. The buckshot was moving up.

He bit his lip, grabbed his coat and started down the steel ladder toward the deck, four bunk heights away. Could he make it up the companionway and out into the fresh air or should he dash straight to the lavatory?—"head" was what his father called it, when he took up a nautical vocabulary

2

and something of a new personality, the moment he climbed aboard their varnish and brass-glistening motor launch. "Head?" an A.B. had mimicked James. "He means the shit-'ouse." The obscenities jarred his senses; not that he hadn't heard most "swear words" by the time he was seven but he and his friends had always uttered these words to each other secretively, with an almost reverent joy.

So many strange names, sounds, smells: human smells, food, garbage, excreta, oil fumes, diesel smoke and the gasping bad breath of forced air vents. Strange humans mainly: grotesques, "oiks"; criminals and murderers for all he knew.

His feet hit the deck.

"Look, there goes that fuckin' Lord Faunt-el-roy again. You'd uv thought he'd coughed his ring up by now."

James, tripping over his overcoat, dashed for the sign: SEAMEN'S W/C.

He was retching into the stale urine smell of the toilet bowl, and, between spasms, he was thinking about the Germans. He had seen plenty of films, both newsreels and war movies and he thought he knew what the Germans were like. He could close his eyes and see Stukas, with evil-shaped wings spitting fire, diving, dropping bombs that screamed like humans under torture. He could see refugees machine-gunned on clogged roads; he could see "the mail-fisted military might of Hitler's hordes" goose-stepping across the world. "Germany calling, Germany calling," boomed over their short-wave radio clearer even than the B.B.C. The mass male-voice choir singing, every night, songs of Germany's invincibleness in march time. (It worried him that he had once found the music magnetizing and had listened to it for hours on end. He found it beautiful and soothing: but that was before he understood.)

He could see the ship being blown up by a torpedo and then he'd be in the water struggling for his life and if he was lucky he'd get in a lifeboat—and then, he thought, horrified, I'll

3

have to go to the bathroom sticking my bare bum over the gunwale and everyone will see me—and then the submarine would surface and machine-gun them all to death.

The day before, his father had put him aboard the tender in Hamilton. He had a new overcoat and a floppy peaked cap. He felt uncomfortable in the cap because it was too big for him; he had never worn a hat before and he was sure he looked silly. He'd been proud of it at first because his father wore one just like it; but now he was on his own among these English people and he couldn't see a hat like his on anybody else's head. He also had on a white shirt, a tie, a new sports coat and a pair of long grey flannels—his first long trousers and he was proud of them. His father had given him a gold tie pin; he wore it just as his father did, holding his collar together under the tie knot.

He had ten pounds in blue Bank of England notes in a chamois leather pouch tied around his stomach, under his vest, with tapes. His father said never to take it off and to James it seemed so large an amount that it could easily incite robbery and murder should its existence become known. He knew he couldn't expect a cabin to himself so he would have to be very careful undressing.

He had a label in his pocket which his father said he must pin on his lapel when he got to "yoo-hoo"—place names never mentioned, "Careless talk costs lives." The label said: JAMES BERKELEY. DELIVER TO: JOHN SOMERS ESQ., 12 BISHOPSGATE, LONDON E.C.2. He hated the thought of wearing this because it would make him look like a baby but he'd promised his father he would and he would.

He had a bunch of green bananas over his shoulder and this made him feel quite ridiculous. "Give them to John Somers," his father had said, "he'll love 'em—they haven't seen bananas for three years."

His father had bought him a ticket on which was written "Stateroom". But, because travel was illegal for civilians, his

4

father had wangled ("Just in case there's a hitch") his being listed as a cabin-boy aged sixteen. His father had "connections" with the Admiralty for whom he built small craft.

The ticket was attached to his passport: "profession student; place and date of birth Bermuda 23 April 1929; colour of eyes blue; colour of hair fair; height 5′ 1″; special peculiarities none." Opposite was his photograph showing his hair standing up like the spikes of a sea-urchin; indeed "Sea-egg" was one of his nicknames.

James understood that if anyone questioned his right to travel he was to refer them to the listing; if they questioned his age, to show them his ticket. "But suppose they question both, Dad?" "They won't. Don't worry. It's just to give them an excuse to wink an eye."

When the tender blew her whistle—a heavy bowel-like sound accompanied by a long and thick plume of pure white smoke—James knew that it was all a mistake. Why hadn't he realized it before? Why? Why am I here?

There was hardly time to think but he knew, as one knows when one has a fever, that he had sinned and that he must pay. He didn't know how he was going to pay, but he knew he must.

The tender cleaved the tranquil greeny-blue water of Hamilton Harbour cutting a white arc as she swung west toward the Great Sound. For a moment she passed but a few feet from the Paget shore—home, a few feet away. He wanted to jump.

He didn't dare look back for the figure of his father; he didn't even dare to look up at their house on the hill. He knew, he thought, only three facts to be certain: that his mother was crazy, that he was a criminal and that he was scared. Beneath this level of consciousness was a great heavy despondency—of his soul, he would have said. It was like an iceberg lodged in his guts, he thought, but he was not sure what caused it. He knew he had felt this feeling before—but when? What was it?

5

There were other people on the tender. James recognized the man who had sold his father the ticket and beyond him other men, some in uniform and some in civvies but all carrying briefcases as well as suitcases. James had no briefcase: a fact that he hoped meant that they wouldn't approach him. He didn't want to talk to anybody. "Berkeleys don't cry," his father said. "Never show emotion in public."

There was a woman too. And although she was much older than he, maybe even eighteen or twenty, she looked frail and unhappy. She must be in one of the women's forces or else some expert or something. But she was pretty and her blue raincoat, tight at the waist, was full at the top from her . . . something? . . . breasts. Rampant was the word: rampant breasts. He didn't know what rampant meant exactly but it was a very exciting word. He tried to see more but the raincoat was too thick. It was bad, sexy, to go peeking at women's breasts but he couldn't help himself. They killed him. Sometimes he couldn't think of anything else and he wished he was an invisible man so that he could just stare, gaze, at them all and no one would know. Then he realized she was smiling at him. He turned away.

They were just passing out of the harbour now and there, not seventy-five yards away, was his uncle's house—pink with a white roof. And there too was the dock and the bathhouses and the diving board. The tender was sucking up a great wave behind her as they entered Two Rock Passage—they always did, tenders and tugs and sometimes a big ship. James and his brothers and cousins would jump in and ride the waves; you could be lifted clear back onto the dock, the wave acting as a billowy elevator. The game then was to keep your feet on the slippery surface as the wave sucked down and away sometimes even exposing the harbour floor: white coral sand, black sea-puddings, purple ferns, brain stones and a few old pop bottles they should have dived up, before tea, last week. Afterwards his aunt always gave them iced tea—with mint leaves, from

6

her garden, green against the yellow, itself smoky with sugar. It was delicious was iced tea with mint; he could remember the first time he'd tasted it.

Through the Passage, the tender turned and soot from the funnel fell on them. Then James saw the two dark-hulled freighters lying at anchor: black and sinister silhouettes against the clear blue of semi-tropical sea and sky. Liberty Ships.

This time his stomach felt as if it had been struck and that its mechanism had stopped: the way you could stop a bicycle wheel by sticking a stick in it. Then he thought he was falling. But he was standing as before and looking around he discovered that no one was looking at him.

He'd imagined the ship would be an armed-cruiser—a liner converted for war-time service—sleek and fast. But these were Liberty Ships. He recognized them at once because a Liberty had been docked in Hamilton a few months before. "Damn ersatz-built hulk," his father had said, "welded, not a rivet in her. The man who dreamed that up ought to be shot."

There must, he thought, be a decent ship around the headland. But he didn't dare hope for that. Did he? No, they were heading straight for the nearest Liberty.

Dad didn't know, he thought. He wouldn't have let me go if he had known. He *couldn't* have.

The ship drew closer. She was very high out of the water and, amidships, she had a towering and frail-looking superstructure which was topped by a thick and seemingly precarious funnel—why didn't it have stays?

They were so close now that he could see that the ship was not dark but pale grey. Gun platforms stuck up from the deck like grotesque pods; the plates in her side, some slightly concave, some slightly convex, looked like painted paper. Not a rivet anywhere.

At least, James noticed, the flag hanging from the stern— already filthy—was the Red Ensign. ("Americans are rotten

7

seamen," his father said. "No discipline at all.") And then they were so close that he could see the streaks of yellow rust, like the patina of over-cooked fried eggs, that ran down her sides.

There were shouts and bangs and the ringing of bells and, before he really knew it, he was on the freighter's slanting deck following the others.

"I say, she's nice and big anyway," James heard a very English voice say.

Then they were sitting in a large room where the chairs were all welded to the deck. James felt that the ship was rolling, slowly, sickeningly, but he knew she wasn't. He waited what seemed a very long time. The woman was called first and then, in turn, each of the men with briefcases. Maybe one of them is a spy?

"Berkeley," a voice shouted out.

The ticket man was standing with an officer. James grabbed up his things and went over. The officer had a face like the photographs of the moon in his grandfather's encyclopaedia. His eyes were small and his blue coat flecked with a strange scale.

"I don't much like this," the officer said, "but if the Old Man—"

"He'll be all right. He comes from a seafaring family. His brother's already in the Navy."

"Air Force, sir," James said but the man wasn't listening. James wanted to explain that he did have another brother who was *going* into the Navy but not until next year when he'd be seventeen ...

"Sign here," the officer gave the agent a look James didn't understand but knew he didn't like and then turned away. James signed. "McIntyre, take care of this lad. Take him below and have Chambers find him a berth."

"Come back, son, when you're settled and let me know how you've made out," said the agent.

8

To James's eyes, children were people and most adults various forms of caricatures of what they once had been. Adults were children deformed: some wrinkled, some hairless, some toothless but all, in some way, bashed about. McIntyre was sort of half-way between the two. He wasn't much taller than James and his face was still young-looking but he had pimples. That meant, James knew, that he could make girls have babies. Also, when McIntyre looked at him, there was an ugly toughness about his eyes that reminded James of crooks in American movies. ("Dramas" they were called and they usually had a man called Garfield in them, or Humphrey Bogart, and they frightened him even more than war movies— but not as much as newsreels. He loved cartoons and some-times he laughed so much he fell off his seat. Best of all was to have two cartoons and then a cowboy double-feature. Ninepence—and when you came out into the sunlight the real world was a gloomy shock and you could keep it away for a while and your bicycle was a horse and you were big and could knock a man down with one punch: the quickest draw in the "terry-tawry" and you shot the bad guy in the stomach and all was right with the world. Tom Mix Berkeley and the Lone Ranger was okay too—he'd rather like to be Tonto, a side kick, because to have a big guy protecting you was great. You could save his life and he'd praise you like anything... but if he was Tom Mix he'd take Gene Autrey's guitar and bash him over the head with it. Movies could make you totally happy—at peace, in heaven—and when you were only allowed one movie a month, to get stuck with a Gene Autrey was like finding a worm in your loquot. But he cheated on the one a month rule; he couldn't help himself, he was always cheating on something. The best movie he had ever seen was called *Destry Rides Again* and the best part was when Destry, who up until then had acted like a real sissy, took the crook's gun and shot six light bulbs off a sign—ke-ke-ke-ke-ke-ke—and how-do-you-like-them-apples?)

9

"What are you anyway," McIntyre said when they were out on deck, "some kind of a fuckin' passenger?"

"I don't really know. I'm on my way to school. But . . . I want to pull my weight on board." (Dad's phrase.) "What do you do?"

"I'm a peggy—not that it's any of your business. Come on then."

On their way aft they passed several seamen idling by the rail.

SEAMEN'S GALLEY. There was a strong smell of stale cooking and garbage: rotten oranges, old tea leaves . . .

"What you got there, Mac, a new mascot for us?"

"I don't know—"

"Cor, stone-the-crows."

"—and 'e don't nyva."

"Whatcha, cock?"

"I beg your pardon?"

"Did you get a load of that piece of skirt, Charlie?"

"'Ark at him. A bloomin toff 'n' all."

"I didn' 'alf."

James in his new black shoes, slipped and almost fell. A hand grabbed him. James looked up. The man, in a dirty apron, smiled at him. James smiled back trying to conceal his fear and repugnance: the man had only two blackened teeth in his mouth and his eyes were strange. "Not quite all there," his mother would have said.

"Na-na, Cookie, mustn't touch."

"Let go of the nipper, you dirty old man."

Laughter.

Chambers, the Bosun, looked James up and down. He put down the penknife with which he had been cutting his nails—with the same action that James's mother used to peel an apple. "Never eat the skins. They have spray on them—besides, you never know who's touched them. Some man who's just done littles and not washed his hands." "Littles" was peeing and it always had been. If he had to spell it he would write littells because, in the family vernacular, defecating was not "bigs" but "grunts"—an ugly word, never to be mentioned outside the family, but familiar also and what was familiar was comforting.

"Cor, love a duck," said the bosun, "what uv we got here?"

James gave his name and said he was on his way to school "and I've a ticket here that my father bought . . . but I expect to work—of course . . . I mean, if there's anything I can do."

Chambers's brow creased so that his bushy eyebrows came together. "Cripes, as if I didn't 'ave enough on me mind." He scratched the side of his head. "With all due respect, mate, your father must be balmy."

"Don't you dare call my father crazy," James wanted to say but all he could manage was what he hoped was a fierce look.

"I've nowhere to put ya, that's all. We've to move aft ourselves, see, to make room for these Admiralty blokes. Well, take 'im below, McIntyre. I'll be down in a jiffy."

"Thank you very much, sir."

Outside again McIntyre turned to him. "Don't you go sucking up to the Bosun. You're no better than the rest of us so stop looking so snotty."

"Laugh," his father had so often said. "You must learn to laugh. You never seem to know when people are kidding you." But James didn't think McIntyre was kidding. Besides, he couldn't remember ever laughing at himself. What was funny about people making fun of you?

No, he thought, far better to try to look tough and keep your dukes up—never mind what you felt inside. He had learned this, by accident, at school. His first term, aged nine, he'd been bullied, almost hopelessly, by other boys. But a master called for volunteers for boxing. James knew a thing or two about boxing; he hadn't been a sparring partner half his life for two elder brothers for nothing. He weighed in "microbe

11

weight" and fought his way clear to the finals cutting down his incompetent windmill opponents with rapid straight jabs. Before a fight he was so scared he had to cross his legs to keep from wetting his pants but when he was in the ring and felt the taut canvas under his sneakers all fear left him—he became "a killer". "Never give in," his elder brother said, "even though you think you're dying. The very next moment your opponent will start bawling." They did or else they got a nose bleed or slipped and pretended they couldn't get up.

He'd even beaten "Ears" Jones, whose ears stuck out like soup ladles, in the finals and "Ears" was the toughest guy in the class. No one had trifled with Berkeley IV after that and the next year "Ears" had died of leukemia and James cried believing that his emotion was grief; for some time he kept sticking pins in himself to make sure his blood was not getting too pale or watery.

But that was kid's stuff and this wasn't.

"Come on then," McIntyre was saying, holding back the heavy canvas blackout curtain.

A blast of thick, evil-smelling hot air came up from below. It was suffocating, sickening and sweet—sweat, smoke. Reaching the bottom of the companionway James felt as if he was buried, trapped. He looked about. Tiers of bunks, men in undershirts, fire axes, signs, steel—everything steel and painted with the same pale, yet dirty-looking grey paint.

"No! No!" a raucous, mocking voice said. "I can't believe it. What is it, a mickey?"

James looked up into the face of a boy about McIntyre's age but taller and with a very prominent Adam's apple. "Perhaps I am," James smiled. "You see at school my nickname was Mickey . . . so, in a way . . ."

"You're right," another seaman said. "You'll be in everybody's fucking way."

Laughter.

James looked about him with what he hoped was a look of

12

pugnacious defiance. Their eyes looked back roving over his new clothes, his suitcase and the bunch of green bananas. Perhaps I'm being rude, he thought, and putting down the suitcase he took off his cap.

"It's Little Lord Fauntelroy 'isself in person."

Laughter.

"Knock-it-off, you blokes. 'Ere mate, you stopping with us? There's a spare bunk up there on top, see? And 'ere's a locker, 'ere, right?"

James hardly dared look his benefactor in the face. Besides, it might be a trick.

"'Ere, lemme 'elp you. It's a long way up but it's nice and cosy."

A few minutes later, James (having put his coat and cap up in the bunk and his suitcase in the locker), desperately needing it, had asked his first question about the whereabouts of the "head".

"Head?" the A.B. said, mimicking him. "He means the shit'ouse." The man, without looking up, gave a jerk of his thumb indicating a steel door behind him.

James pushed against the heavy spring. Then, to his horror, he was confronted with six toilet bowls, in a row without partitions of any kind. On one a man was seated, his trousers at his ankles revealing white and incredibly hairy knees.

"Come on in, the water's fine," the man said.

James let the spring push both the door closed and himself out again.

"What's with you, Faunty-boy, bashful?" It was McIntyre.

Laughter.

James pushed again and went in. The stench of excreta was nauseating.

"Come on then," the man said smiling.

Feeling both the heavy weight of claustrophobia and an agony of shyness James stood before a toilet, but, knowing the man was looking at him, he could not pee.

13

"You oughta whistle, mate. That'll do it."

James stood and stood and then he made an elaborate show of shaking as if the job was done.

When he turned the seaman was looking the other way.

James thought that if he could wait until dark he could sneak upstairs and pee over the rail.

Back in the crew's quarters he found the place surprisingly empty—only McIntyre and three or four others. He could not see the man who had helped him. Then he noticed that McIntyre was going through his suitcase.

"Cor, look at this."

James rushed towards him. "Put that down."

"Gur-cha, nipper. 'Oo's this?"

"My sister," James said and grabbed for it.

McIntyre deftly swung it out of his reach. "Cor, whatta looka. Does she fuck?"

"Stop that," James said trying to be stern yet hearing, with despair, the squeak of his own voice, "she's only thirteen."

"I'm not superstitious," a voice called out. "Does she nip and tuck?"

Laughter.

James thought of his sister with her pigtails and skinny arms and her little breasts that pushed out her sweater like two tiny tents held up with matchsticks; he always tried not to look at them but his eyes seemed to have a heavy will of their own.

"Of course she does." McIntyre shoved his face, pimples and dirty-looking yellow fuzz, close to James. "Look at 'im blushin'. 'E's been fucking 'er isself, the dirty little snob."

"Berkeley," a voice called out from above.

McIntyre dropped the folder. James grabbed it and shoved it in his suitcase. He locked the case, his hands moving with a sort of angry and panicked precision.

"Berkeley!"

"Coming, sir." James stowed the suitcase and then ran up the companionway to the deck.

14

It was the shipping agent. "There you are. All settled? Comfortable?"

James wanted to beg the man to take him away. It was his last chance.

"Don't you want me to tell your father you are comfortable and happy?"

At the mention of his father James couldn't speak. Comfortable? Happy? He could feel the agent's impatience to be gone. Then, anger at what he took to be the man's base treachery and deceit rose up and choked him. Stateroom?

"Come along, lad. You don't want your mother and father to worry, do you?"

"—" James managed a nod and then turned away.

"That's a good lad. I'll tell them."

After a few moments James heard the man's footsteps clanging metallically down to the tender.

The day before, at home lying on the counterpane of his mother's cedar four-poster (in which, he knew, generations and generations of the family had been born: all the way back to the first Faith—his great-grandmother? Anyway, the frail and beautiful one, who had died giving birth to her thirteenth child—and probably before), with his trunk open on the floor and all his clothes laid out, he had listened to her voice on the phone downstairs.

"Your concern is most touching, Daisy." His mother's voice was different when she talked on the phone, a sort of very theatrical timbre, an arched Englishness took over. It was quite unlike her normal voice and to think of his mother as being dishonest or phoney—or trying *not* to think so—always gave him a slight headache. ". . . but I can assure you that George and I have given the matter great and *soul*-searching thought—"

She was talking about him, he knew, and it was also quite obvious that she was getting angry. Daisy was his godmother.

He liked his "Aunt Daisy" because she was rich and beautiful and moved like a longtail gliding. She never got rattled and people made a big fuss over her, bowing and scraping and calling her Lady Sheringham. Best of all she really *liked* him, he believed—she gave him a whole pound every Christmas. "Well, George, as a former naval officer should surely know better than anyone else—" "No, he thinks it's absolutely safe —" "Yes. It's kind of you to say we have courage but Daisy the truth is—" "Mad, I should say we are very much *not* mad—" "For that matter, Daisy, let me tell you that I'd sooner have a dead son than an alive, *spoiled, Americanized Bermudian juvenile delinquent*." Sound of the phone being banged onto the hook. Sound of his mother sighing.

Any moment, he knew, she'd be making one of her pleas to heaven: "Oh, angels help women." She wasn't really crazy he told himself, she was just exhausted from, as she said, "bearing five children and slaving after six—my eldest being your father." James felt very guilty about his mother. His parents were always fighting and he always took his father's side. He felt that he had betrayed his mother and betrayed her very often. He didn't know why he had betrayed her but he thought it just must be that he was bad, rotten. He liked to tell himself that she really did pick on his father; he liked to think that his father was always in the right the way he, James, said he was but deep down he knew he wasn't. He always backed him up ("Back me up, Jamie, I never said that, did I?") right or wrong so that he would like him more than the others. That was it, he thought, and it was bad, wicked.

James, that first day on board, lay in his bunk thinking of his father's bunk in the little bedroom down the long hall from his mother's room. (He'd just made a startlingly relieving discovery: at certain times the crew's quarters became, for God knew what reason, almost deserted, and then one had a sporting chance of having the bathroom to oneself. He'd had a great

16

pee—he wanted to go grunts too but he didn't dare take down his pants, that was too risky.) Dad slept by himself, he knew, because he had nightmares of the first war. Also, his mother liked her sheets tight and the old man couldn't even bear to have his covers tucked in. "It was the war," he said, "you had to be able to get out quickly. To jump when the alarm went." His father had been "over the side" three times. Once he'd been the only survivor. His father was a hero and was very brave. Christopher, his elder brother, was very brave too, and Teddy was brave and James was becoming more and more sure each minute that he was a complete coward.

He pulled his overcoat over him. His father's bunk was nothing like this one, not steel and skinny but varnished mahogany and baronial. Best, it stood on the floor and was not perilously high up as this one was. James realized that his was the furthest bunk from the companionway. He had, in an emergency, to get all the way down and then across the floor before he even started up towards the deck. Maybe he should practise? Would there be a mad scramble? As the littlest he would be the worst off in a scramble and the ship might sink before he got out.

He touched the steel of the side of the ship and imagined a torpedo like a great penis coming through. But, of course, you wouldn't see it—you'd be blown up. Then he heard the men coming back.

Kling, kling. Kling, kling. Kling, kling.
3.00 his watch said.
"Loud-speakers. Jesus Christ, 'oo'd uv ever thought I'd serve on a ship without a decent clock even. It's proper weird —don't sound *decent*."
"Gives me the creeps."
"Is it right the Old Man's got a woman in his cabin?"
James recognized the voice. The one with the Adam's apple. Hammersmith, they called him.

"Yeah. I saw 'er. Smashin bit o' skirt."

"Christ. 'Ow does 'e do it? Two cabins and now a woman."

"She's a fuckin' passenger, you idiot."

"You can say that again." It was Harry, the A.B. who'd helped him up that first climb to his bunk. He hadn't been very friendly since then; it was as if he was ashamed that he ever had been.

"No. Knock it off. I mean it. She's married to an R.A.F. bloke in Blighty."

"Coo. I wish I was in the R.A.F. 'Ome every night. No water—"

"She's the Skipper's tart. I bet she is."

"Imagine. 'Ome every night. And if you do 'ave to fly over the water you don't have to be *in* it all the bleedin' toim."

"Yeah. That stinkin' captain. I bet he's bangin' 'er blind."

"The lucky fucker."

"You can say that again."

"Hofficers," said Hammersmith with disgust. "Hofficers, I shits 'em."

"Fuck the captain."

"You can say that again."

"Fuck the captain."

"After you with the captain, mate." Harry.

James lay curled up in his bunk, not moving, feeling his own warm breath come back at him from the blanket half covering his face. He felt lost, lonely and ill. It was homesickness: that was what his mother had said had been the matter that night he had stayed at his cousin's house when he was nine. He'd liked being there in the daylight and he and his cousin played quite happily. But then it grew dark and James, with his supper plate in front of him, did not feel hungry at all. It was, he thought, because the food was strange and because he missed his home. Later, in bed, he could not sleep. It was no good asking his cousin's parents if he could go home—

they might not let him saying he had no light for his bike. No, he'd have to escape. He got dressed with the utmost stealth. (His cousin's father was a fierce and short-tempered man. "He can't help it," his mother said, "he went through absolute *Hell* in the trenches.") Climbing out of the window onto the veranda he made his way to where the bicycles were stored under the house. The moon was bright outside but the cellar door was in shadow. Maybe he should just run for it? No, that would mean he'd have to come back for the bicycle the next day and he didn't want to face these people again.

He only knew he *had* to get home and if he got there he'd never leave again. The screened cellar door was hooked on the inside. It was a criminal thing to do, he knew, but he took out his penknife and made a slit in the screen. He was always doing criminal things, he thought—he just didn't seem to be able to help himself.

He got the door open silently and he got his bike silently, but then, in his haste, he let the door slip and bang. The dog started barking. James jumped on his bike and pedalled down the drive as fast as he could.

He heard his uncle calling after him but he sped on. The shadows of the trees frightened him; fear of the dark and ghosts frightened him but not as much as he was frightened of his uncle and he wasn't nearly as frightened of his uncle as he was of—what was it? That he might never get home; that his home might not be there when he got there. No, that was ridiculous; it was, he thought, simply that he loved his home so much that he couldn't stand being away.

At home everyone was, to his surprise, very kind. His mother even said that his uncle had called and asked that he not be punished. He understood, he said. Wait till he finds the screen, James thought.

His mother tucked him in bed and he was very happy to have so much attention. He had never, he said, left home before and he was never going to again.

19

But when the light was out he remembered the cold and "beastly" (his sister called it, quite rightly he thought) school they had gone to in Bognor when his mother was "sick" in the nursing home and his father away "on business". He was five and his sister six and every night when the matron had put out the light he'd climb in his sister's bed and they would hold each other and cry—but he had to be careful not to fall asleep there or you got "the slipper" in the morning. He could not bear to leave her side but when she was asleep he did. Once, he'd wet her bed; he woke up. She was asleep. In the morning he let them give her the slipper without "owning-up". Half-way through, when she started to cry (how could she last so long when he always bawled after the first whack?), he couldn't stand it any more and said it was he who'd done it. They didn't believe him and said he was "an angel" to protect her like that. It only made it twice as bad.

That night at home, after his cousin's, he'd pulled the covers over his head (he always did that every night because he was afraid of ghosts) and now, on board the boat, he was doing it again.

He fell asleep. When he woke up he thought he was home. But the ship's humming and the total greyness everywhere ... He gasped and looked about. The crew's quarters was empty except for one grey-haired old seaman. The man looked kindly so James climbed down and said:

"I beg your pardon but I'm new. Do you know what my duties are to be?"

The man sighed. "Just keep your bloomin' 'ead out of port-holes, that's all, matey."

What could he mean, James wondered? The ship didn't seem to have any portholes.

He went to the head, which he found empty, and when he came out the man said, "You wanta go and have some grub, that's what you should do."

"This is the B.B.C. Overseas Service," blared the loud-speakers. "Klang, klong, kling, klang . . ." Big Ben, at home Dad would be listening, having a whisky and soda.

"I'm not hungry." The feeling in his stomach again—"ho-hum ta-tum," James said to himself, "I'm going to be sick."

"Here is the news: elements of the British Army today engaged . . ."

"Na, look, matey. You look pale. What ya need is a little grub—some char, anyway. You don't want the other lads laughing at ya, do ya?"

". . . on a wide sector so far undisclosed . . ."

Even the B.B.C. could not drown out the heavy sound of the vents and the ominous hum of generators. He'd never imagined that ships made so much noise.

James looked at the yellow mess of eggs and soggy toast in front of him. So this was supper: "tea" the men called it. He tried to drink the hot tea. It was sickeningly sweet. Ho-hum, ta-tum.

Hammersmith's chin had a dirty-looking fuzz on it. Why didn't he shave? "Don't you want your eggs? You seasick already?"

"No, just not hungry," James said smiling. He felt very shy and self-conscious—as if he was naked—and wished he'd stayed in his bunk. He did not understand them; their world was very strange yet he knew he must, somehow, win their favour . . . or perish. He smiled again. "You can have half each if you like."

"Tar," Hammersmith said, grabbing the plate.

Hammersmith ate with what was, to James, incredible violence. He put his head down low to the plate and shovelled the food into his mouth—loud smacks and sucking noises. One hand high on his knife so that his fingers were on the blade, the other closed in a fist over the fork.

James was repelled and wondered, for a moment, if these people were like coloured people, inferior, a different species.

21

"You trying to suck up to us?" McIntyre asked.

The smile that had been lingering on James's mouth, shrank.

"You're a bleeding arse'ole creeper, that's what you are."

James pretended he didn't hear. He took a sip of the tea in the thick white cup. Sickly sweet but strangely bitter from the canned milk.

"Leave 'im be," someone said. "'E's not doing you no 'arm."

He pinched his own leg under the table to keep back his tears. He knew he could often keep from crying when being attacked but sympathy could open the flood-gates. Anger could do it too.

He remembered once losing a fight against a Portuguese boy—an "oik"—because he got angry. James had tried to rescue (Sir Galahad Berkeley) the puppy the boy appeared to be choking with a lead made out of string. In the ensuing fight the boy had kicked his shins and righteous indignation at such cheating, flaunting the Marquis of Queensberry's rules, rose up and choked James. He had flayed out blinded by his own tears and the boy had tripped him and kicked him again as he went down. James had been left with an anger compounded with the hangover rage that the other boy did not know why he'd burst into tears and never would. He *hadn't* given in . . . but had he?

Now he was going to be sick. He jumped up with his hand over his mouth, dodged by "Cookie" (who he fleetingly realized must have been his ally) and banged into the water-tight door. Cookie opened it and somehow propelled James out of it.

He made it to the side. He was sick into the darkness of the sea below. He retched everything out of his stomach. Then he retched the resulting emptiness until stars popped inside his eyeballs. He could not stop.

Slowly the retching subsided and then he became aware

that he was bitterly cold. They were still in Bermuda but it seemed that the coldness of England had already reached out and grabbed them. His coat was below.

Then, suddenly, the air he breathed seemed mysteriously pure and fresh—more refreshing than he had ever before known air could be. He hadn't really thought of air as existing before.

It's an alive thing, he thought. What would happen if it died?

He ought to get his coat. His mother had said to always wear his coat on deck, for walks, and to be sure to do up the top button. He made his way aft. Reaching the hooded entrance to the crew's quarters he thought he heard, out of the darkness, a woman's laughter, high and bubbling. There it was again; he felt a deep longing and then, in the next instant, utterly bereft.

The hot blast from below hit him and he rushed back for the rail.

Later he found a somewhat sheltered hiding place between the afterdeck house—on which was perched the 3″ gun—and a large wooden raft.

When the cold became greater than his fear that he would be sick again if he did go, he went below and climbed in his bunk.

"I should'uv stayed in Trinidad. One of me mates got a smashin' job there working for the Yanks. Yea, ten quid a week."

"'E won't 'alf cop it when they catch 'im."

"Na. 'E's changed 'is name. 'E's a proper—what do you call it—mimic. Talks like a real West Indian."

"He'll cop it. You gotta 'ave an Identity Card, 'aven't you."

"Where've you been? In Port-of-Spain you could buy the Duke of Windsor's passport for ten bob."

"I don't like it." Harry. *Harry*.

23

"What are you drippin' about now, Smith. You don't like nothing."

"I tell you. I don't like a bucket with a dead ship's name."

Someone was winding a watch.

See-saw ticking. His grandmother had a little gold watch pinned to her sweater; his sister and he would crawl under the piano and listen to her play Chopin. His sister always hugged her knees, closed her eyes and was quite still. When Grandmother played Bach, Grandfather sometimes accompanied her on the banjo. It gave him a very cosy feeling when they played together but Bach was not as beautiful as Chopin —it was, as his sister said, the pauses in Chopin that killed you.

"Name ain't nothing." Hammersmith.

"A lot you know, sprog. Get some sea-time in. When you've been over the side three times then you can talk."

Dad. Oh God, Dad, come and take me away. If you listen very hard you can hear me. Telepathy. If you love me you'll hear—you have to.

"'E's right. This ship's a bad one."

"Yeah," Harry, "she'd roll scuppers under in the Serpentine on a Sunday in May. I had a talk with that R.N. Chief yesterday. 'E figures in a blow—even a little one—she'd turn turtle as quick as winking. 'E says the Old Man's gonna put us all in the boats if it dusts up."

"That bleedin' Captain." McIntyre. "'Im and his whisky —'e's 'alf pissed all the time."

"You leave the Old Man alone, you snivelling little peggy." It was Chambers. James raised his head a little. Chambers stood, legs apart, holding a life jacket in his hand. "If anyone can get us to England, mate, 'e can."

"'Oo says we're going to England?"

"Chrissake. Ask Lord Faunteroy—even he knows that much. Doncha, Faunty?" Chambers looked up, winked and then swung the life jacket in his hand. "Berkeley. Keep this jacket with you all the time. And I mean all the time. I never want to see it off you except when in your sack and then it's to be under your head. Got me?"

"Yes." He tried not to move his head very much: his mother always said if you lie very still you won't throw up.

"Tomorra there'll be a drill—"

"Oh Christ's-muvva-Mary."

"Not again."

"We've drilled all the way from Baltimore—"

"Those weren't drills—they was Jerry—"

"Shut up. And Smith—you show Berkeley the ropes. 'E gets into trouble and I'll 'ave *you*—you understand?"

Chambers left.

"Harry," Hammersmith said with quiet concern, "do you think we'll make it?"

"Mr. Smith to you, sprog."

"Turn-it-tup. I'm serious."

"'Ow would I know if we're going to make it? But I'll tell you one thing. I'm not taking my clothes off on this ship—not even for a shower. *Empire United* indeed. Luck of this ship we'll draw an outside berth in a convoy of Greeks—all of 'em able to make three knots only when they're belching smoke worse than the Battersea Power Station. Yeah, outside berth on the sunny side. Do you know what the sunny side going 'ome means, 'Ammersmith?"

"No."

"Well, cock, let's 'ope the fucking Jerries are as young and dumb as you then."

And he was retching into the bowl and the strong smell of man-pee came up at him, kept gagging him. "Keep your head out of portholes." And overhead the deck sounded alive—footsteps and the clanging and crashing of equipment. "Sunny side going home"—if he didn't stop being sick he'd have no strength left.

Ka-rung, ka-rung, ka-rung.

25

Noise like a train with a broken wheel. He'd heard it so often before in Hamilton Harbour. Anchor chain? Yes. They were bound for sea—he was "going to sea". Going to sea, going to sea.

Shra-a-gronk-orank-orank-orank.

Silence. "Number Three boat on the Port side, Berkeley, and don't you forget it." "When the alarm bell goes look sharp —get to your station by that locker and keep out of the bleedin' way."

Ka-rung, ka-rung, ka-rung.

"I'm not taking any clothes off this trip . . . " Me either. I've got to stop throwing up. I've got to get on deck.

He tried lying flat on his back on the steel floor. His mother sometimes put a cool wash-cloth on his forehead. He must get on deck. It would be dark now: just gone six and everyone's "tea" had been delayed. If he could get on deck he could see the lights of Bermuda and maybe there was still a chance he could get off. His father would come roaring out in the motor boat and stop the ship and take him home. "Get my son. Berkeley is his name. James Berkeley. Get my boy."

But he didn't believe it. They were bound for sea. The ship was moving. He heard the noises of the capstan and the screw —dirty word. The capstan and the screw and now the screw was saying: down-to-the-sea, down-to-the-sea.

Then the ship trembled and gave a great shudder and the screw stopped and then started again with a new sound. Going astern, James knew, and the new sound said: Mum-mum-mum-mum.

He got up and ran cold water on his handkerchief and touched it to his face. He'd get on deck even if he had to be sick all the way.

His bedroom window faced west and overlooked the harbour. The warm sun set in the west; all ships that sailed from Hamilton sailed west so that he had thought of all places—

England, America, everywhere—as being west. West, too, was up: warm, hopeful and full of bright prospects.

But now, standing on the deck in the cold darkness as the *Empire United* dieseled down the channel—with the lights of Bermuda twinkling on his right—he realized that they were pointing almost east. England, of course, was north-east; how could he have been so stupid? The ships sailed west simply because the harbour's mouth was west. Remember Bognor, England's cold. And East was down; north, cold. They were not sailing up towards the warm but down, down, he thought, to hell. Hell was cold like the air coming off the sea—the bitter cold of England reaching out . . . But the shore was still so close. The lights twinkling, cheerful in contrast to the ship's blacked-out gloom. No one in Bermuda bothered about the black-out any more—this wasn't 1940, it was '42.

Ga-vum, ga-vum, ga-vum . . .

Then, approaching St. George's, the easternmost part of the islands, the channel brought them even closer to the shore. I could jump, James thought, I could swim that far. He looked down at the black and heavy sea upon which the ship's monstrous bulk (the sides as sheer as the walls of his father's warehouse) carved wakes—rolling white waves trailing off to foam . . . It was awfully far down.

It's my last chance, James thought, and I've jumped from higher places. Then he remembered the ship's propeller—he might be sucked in and chopped to pieces. It would be better to dive—dive as far out as possible and then swim for all he was worth. But the ship was moving—the momentum might break his back when he hit the water. He should turn, at the last minute, he calculated, and hit the water facing forward like an arrow.

Immediately he imagined the expression of disappointed displeasure on his father's face. I could not hurt Dad that much, he thought. If he lost the approval of his father he would have lost everything.

With a sinking spasm of despair, which registered in his stomach in a painful sort of convulsion ("You've a weak stomach—just like your father" his mother always said) he realized that it was too late. The time to turn back had been noon yesterday before the agent left—no, it was too late then. He should have got off the tender in Hamilton—but it was too late then too. When should he have got off? Surely he hadn't always been destined to end up on this ship?

The *Empire United*, an automaton monster seemingly controlling, not controlled by, the crew or even the captain, throbbed on, the superstructure rolling against the barely discernible stars beyond which was blackness and then more blackness. (He remembered that, years before, one night he'd asked his parents what was beyond the stars. More stars, they said. And beyond them? No one knows. And he had gone out in the garden and looked up and thought with *all his might*. But he could not figure it out: what was beyond the beyond? He had banged his head against the impregnable wall where the chimney towered up appearing to move, with the clouds—but his brain would not give him the answer.) The thick funnel gasped out fumes that poisoned the air.

Silence. The engine had stopped. James leaned over the side and watched the ship's phosphorescent wash slowly reduce to a black bubble-flecked whisper. In the background he heard the humming of the vents and then some shouting and the sharp hammering of running boots on the steel deck.

Out of the night came the twinkling red eye of the tiny wooden pilot boat, nursing towards the ship's hull much as a baby sucker-fish might approach a whale.

A gossamer shiver of warm happiness tingled down his back. The little boat was home: his father had built all the pilot boats and built them strong, sturdy ("triple-planked mahogany and all copper and brass fastened"), proud. Then, as the little boat drew nearer, rolling and pitching like a child's top, he

28

could hear the shouts of the Negroes who manned her—sounds so Bermudian, so familiar . . .

He had forgotten about the pilot until now: here was his chance. He could dive in now. The coloured men would fish him out and gladly restore him safe to his father.

"Get that Jacob's ladder up here." The Bosun. James checked the tapes on his life-jacket.

Jump? What about his trunk? His suitcase? The family had spent more than they could afford on equipping him. But he *had to get home*. Surely the coloured men would understand and help him.

Then he realized that it was not so likely. More likely they would fish him out and the captain would shout through a megaphone and have him hauled on deck again. Then he would have to face punishment, embarrassment, ridicule—they might even flog him.

It was useless.

James watched the blue-uniformed pilot approach the ladder. The dim light struck silver streaks on his brown face.

"Sure you wouldn't loik a nice cruise to Blighty?" Harry, the joker.

"No, thank you—fact-of-the-matter—" the man laughed the high pealing laugh James had heard so often. He never asked himself exactly what it meant he only knew that white men never laughed that way. "Fact-of-the-matter, gentlemen, I *been* there. See over there." He pointed, "my wife and kiddies over there right on that heel—you're going to yours but mine's right over there waitin'." He laughed again and started to climb the gunwale.

James wanted to run up to him. He didn't know the man but the man would know his name when he gave it. He wanted to run up if only for the benediction of one last soft unjudging Bermudian Negro voice. "Good luck, sonny," the man would say with that frowning smile with which all coloured people, it seemed, looked at white people. "Good luck, Mr. Berkeley," he might even say and thus give him one last push towards the courage he knew he didn't possess.

The pilot would talk about his family, his father, the boats, his brothers—they always know everything, James thought, even when you don't know them, they know you and all about you—and the crew would hear . . .

But he stayed in his hiding place by the life-raft and watched the pilot climb down the swaying Jacob's ladder. The shouts from below sounded so relaxed, so happy—well may they be happy, they are going home.

When the ship started forward again he knew that he was caught, doomed, powerless against the grip of what appeared to be a black monster called Fate.

He saw that there was nothing he could do to resist this awful force; he had always been bound to end up on this ship destined towards a future it took all his strength to keep from imagining.

He knew he was being punished for his sins. He knew he was going to PAY. For what were the worst sins? Lying? Yes, he lied all the time and always had done. Stealing? He had stolen even from his mother's purse—a whole pound—*his own mother* and the gardener was fired. Swearing? Yes. Not working at school? He had always done as little work as he could get away with doing. He threw his homework books in the oleander bushes and told his mother he didn't have any homework. He always half-expected that she wouldn't believe him but she always did—in fact she didn't even seem to be listening. What else? Disloyalty, Jew-baiting, murder and sex.

He was disloyal to his own people nearly every time he talked to Negroes—he did it just so they would like *him*. In his gang at school he was the ring-leader at Jew-baiting; he made the gunpowder himself. "Jew-crackers", he called them and thrown under a bicycle they scared hell out of little Jewish kids.

He hadn't committed murder but sex was his biggest crime because it was with him all the time. Besides, he thought, if anyone knew what he and Charlie (the lower-class boy he was forbidden to play with—another thing) had done in Paget marsh, he'd have to kill them before they could squeal. Charlie's thing was as big as a thick sausage and his was very small. When he rubbed Charlie's he could put his whole hand around it and there was room for one more hand. He rubbed it up and down and it felt hard and fibrous—it was enormous. To rub his, Charlie could only use two fingers and a thumb, reaching down as if he was picking up marbles—it was too small for anything else. Charlie said that his would get big too: but James didn't believe it would get that big. His mother was right, Charlie really was an "oik": he was ugly (even uglier than he was and he knew he was the ugliest member of his family—his mother had said so) and coarse. Why do working class boys always get bigger things—able to make babies—sooner than we do? Sex was evil: therefore they are more evil than us. But his mother was right, he shouldn't have played with Charlie. At nine (Charlie was two years older) Charlie had told him that men stuck their things in women's behinds and that's how women got babies. It seemed reasonable, exciting and disgusting: pretty awful thing to be grunted into this world. It took him two years to find out that men went in the front: exciting too but the former, the earlier imagined sin, fired his imagination the more. They were ten and twelve when they "tried it out": they took turns but it never worked. But once, when Charlie had his between James's legs, Charlie had thought he was "in". "Am I in?" "Yes", lied James. Charlie had withered. "I didn't hurt you, did I?" Charlie was scared but he was concerned too. James could tell that: Charlie really cared. That was the funny thing about Charlie; he could surprise you by being a very nice person. That was why it hurt to have to be always telling him that he couldn't come to Westhill; he couldn't even come in the gate of the driveway—it was forbidden. Charlie's father was a fat, stunted cripple in a wheelchair. Their cottage smelled, sickeningly, of cooking—

31

cod-fish. His father did the cooking; his mother worked in a store.

The lights of Bermuda were lower now and some of them seemed to go out and then come on again: it was the waves rising and falling, he knew that. The sea hiding the lights of home. James went and stood at the very stern of the ship. He grasped the cold rail in his hands and heard the strap, strap of the small halyard against the empty flag-staff. Flag-staff bereft of its flag: it made him feel sick again.

The ship's wake trailed off astern, an undulating white road with its centre tossed up in an endless chain of white rooster's tails. Gu'vum, gu'vum, gu'vum, ground the engine and the propeller blades thumped the water, one after the other, with a sound much like he and his friends used to make when they jumped from the high diving board seeing who could make the biggest splash—bombshells, they called it. *Gah-vumb, gah-vumb.*

Then a strange feeling came over him. He felt as if he was being watched: as if he was in the ring or on stage. For a moment it didn't seem unlikely that God himself was watching. Then it was as if he floated upwards out of his body and was looking down at it.

Crash!

A man was dumping garbage. The flotsam floated away with surprising speed and when he followed one box out of sight he saw that Bermuda had gone too.

A flash of light. Turning, James saw the man lighting the stub of a cigarette. The face was hollow-cheeked, gaunt and grey stubble grew on the jaw.

"Put out that bleedin' fag." Chambers. Chambers was everywhere. "You know better than that—Jerry could see that ten miles away."

"All right. All right."

"It's not all right—that's just what it isn't."

"Nark, nark."

"And that's the last garbage you dump too—haven't you read the orders? You want to get me in dutch with Mr. Billings, I suppose?"

"It was Mr. Billings 'isself told me dump," the man shuffled off, his voice a discontented whine. "So *thou* can shove that up . . ."

"Berkeley, is that you?"

"Yes."

"You stopped being sick yet, mate?"

"Well . . . I hope so."

"Well you betta 'ad. Can't 'ave you snappin' your biscuits all the way 'ome, now can we?"

"Suppose not." Home?

"You're right, nipper. So you just keep stopped—or I'll 'ave to give you the Cure." Chambers laughed and walked away.

The Cure. Perhaps I wouldn't feel so bad, he thought, if I went to the bathroom. Like when you have a stomach upset— sometimes you aren't sick if it goes out the other end. He didn't want to be sick and he didn't want the Cure and his bowels ached for relief but none of these things out-weighed his fear of being seen—discovered—with his pants down "going grunts". He was more afraid of this than he was of German submarines.

But then, when he looked out at the rolling sea, he thought that what he was most afraid of was that—the sea. The sea was so vast, so unfathomably deep. To drown would be a horrible death: down down down. To suffocate in that ghastly, cold vastness.

Ocean, oh-shun, ocean, oh-shun . . .

What the fuck, he asked himself, was so fuck fucking funny about fucking life? And then he looked up at the sky hoping God hadn't heard him.

II

It was right, he thought, what his mother said: he was a juvenile delinquent.

Kling, kling. Kling, kling . . . eight bells. Every eight bells was a watch change, he'd found out. Midnight. He hoped he wouldn't be put on watch. He was sick, after all. But if Chambers—who he'd been ducking all night—found him he'd get the Cure. He lay very low and still in his bunk hoping it would look as if he wasn't there.

They were at convoy stations now. Their sister ship, the Commodore ship, they called her, in the middle; a big tanker to port, west; themselves to starboard, east—down, he thought again. Cold and dark on their side—but at least west was the sunny side, wasn't it? H.M.S. *Charybdis* ahead, low and grey —everything had been grey when he left his hiding place on deck just before dark. The sky and sea a pale cold and weak grey as if the very elements had lost their strength. What could grow here? Nothing. All was bleak and barren; like the moon.

If you were on the moon you'd suffocate. He imagined himself dropped, stranded on the moon. He wondered if he'd have even time to carve his name on a rock, with his penknife, before he suffocated—drowned, but at least he would be on land not the awful sea.

"She looks business-like anyway, that Charribus," Hammersmith had said.

"Should've been scrapped twenty years ago, the bleedin' old cripple." Harry.

"You're a fine one, calling one of 'Is Majesty's destroyers a cripple." One of the R.N. ratings. "You should ought to be grateful the Royal Navy's takin' care of ya, cock."

"Get stuffed." Harry, laughing. "The fuckin' Royal Navy gives me a pain. Bunch of sailor boys in blue and gold. Christ-almighty, the Merchant Marine is at sea all the time and then once every twenty years you R.N. baskets come out and get all the medals."

"'Ere Bob, china. You want to come over 'ere and 'ear the lip Oi'm takin' from a chancred-up old sea-cook."

"But what I mean is, I'd like to be on that destroyer." Hammersmith, serious. "I mean, it's like in trouble you can get away in'it? Fast 'n' all. And then again, I bet she don't roll like this bastard."

"Coo, 'ark-at-'im." The rating. "You wanta try destroyers, mate. I'll-tell-ya. Roll! Dive! Fuckin'-arse'oles. I was on destroyers with the 'Ome Fleet—Scapa—'38. Christ, I'll tell you, we was tyin' each uvver in our 'ammocks. Bashed every which way. Just from the jarrin'—poundin'—you'd split your kidneys.

"My kidneys give me 'ell, see. So first leave I got I swiped me old woman's corset. Worked out smashin'. Strapped me up real good. Wish I could've seen me old woman's face when she found out. Cor, she musta bin proper chocka—lovely old thing, best toim for a slap and tickle is when she's chocka. Laugh, I could've pissed meself—and then this fuckin' pip-squeak of a one-striper made me take it off. Destroyers, mate, you can 'ave 'em—polishin' brass standin' on your fuckin' 'ead. 'Ere, Bob, you Geordie sod, where are ya?"

James had all his clothes on—but he'd slipped off his shoes —and his blanket and overcoat over him. He felt alternately

35

too cold and too hot. The place fell quiet again but the wire-caged lights, in the centre of the ceiling, stayed on. They always did.

But, yes, he had been a juvenile delinquent. It had started, hadn't it, with Guy Fawkes Day? Gunpowder. No more fire-crackers after war broke out. O.K. he'd make his own. Grand-father's study at Cedar Hill had an *Encyclopaedia Britannica*.

"Studying, Benjamin?" Grandfather always calling him by his middle name, the crazy old guy. "That's a good boy. What is it you're after?"

Quick look at opposite page. "Gunnery, naval, Grampy." Wow, hope that isn't vulgar, dirty. No, Grandfather wanders off.

Lot of junk about whether the British or the Germans invented it first . . . here we are, a table of recipes by countries and dates. The most modern was 1882 and it was German. Since the Germans are the baddest people their recipe will be the best. Saltpetre 78, charcoal 19, sulphur 3. Zowie.

Money? Well, his precious comic books (strictly forbidden and utterly delicious, sheer heaven to read secretly in the garden) would have to go. Forbidden? How, he wondered in his bunk, had he managed to collect over a hundred of them? Stealing and cheating, that was how.

Superman and Planet stuff would have to go: he'd graduated to Batman and Captain America anyway. The crooks were more awful and inventive and even tortured beautiful girls who had bursting big breasts—but they never went far enough.

What seemed like layer after layer of his fathomless evil came back to him: it was not only the sex, he had found him-self wishing, more and more often, that the crooks would win. Why should they always be caught? Wham! Pow! Tear her clothes right off.

Superman gone and over eight shillings hot in his pocket. Pile's Drugstore. Old "Smile" Pile himself sold him a package of saltpetre. Charlie suggested, rightly, not to buy all the ingredients in one shop. At the Phoenix Mr. Sousa looked suspicious but handed over two shillings worth of sulphur to Charlie—it was his turn.

Feeling like bank robbers they hurried up the hill to the Pharmaceutical Hall. "Good thing there's only three things in it," said Charlie, "there's only three drug stores."

German recipe or not it didn't work. Fumfpt! went the toilet paper wrapped ingredients. Fumfpt.

It had been his cousin Edmund, he remembered, who had solved the problem. Edmund was weak and bad, his mother said. James thought she was probably right and that he and Edmund were similar. "Poor Edmund," his mother said, "deserted by his mother and his father sick—a weakling too, he can't help it." Which meant, James knew, that his uncle was a drunk. But James and his sister liked that uncle best because he was generous: generosity was their basic measure of a person's goodness.

Edmund was ten years older than he was and should have volunteered like Christopher and gone to England. But Edmund had accepted conscription in the local forces and spent his time guarding the Cable and Wireless Company's towers. He'd shot a billy goat one dark night by mistake. They said it was disgraceful for a Berkeley to be a common private along with a lot of Portuguese and white trash. Edmund only smiled shyly and said he'd do his best to make lance-corporal. Later, he'd sing James the march of the Bermuda Rifle Corps. "Forty thousand Portuguees coming through the trees..." Edmund was funny and if he was a "wastrel" he was also very talented. He could play the mouth-organ—any tune you could name—and he could whistle two notes at one time. And Edmund had solved the gunpowder problem: "Weigh it— measuring isn't accurate enough."

James, lying in the bunk, remembered that it had been Edmund who had first initiated them, years ago, into the forbidden joys of goo-goos. He and his sister were still little then.

What had Edmund said? Just something about rubbing yourself "down-there" until it felt "good-good-good-GOO-GOO'S!" "No, I won't tell you any more—told you too much already. And if you little kids tell on me I'll—I'll send my demons after you."

They were naughty—bad—to have listened to Edmund. That very night they'd done it. Lying in their separate beds, face down, they'd rubbed their "littles" against the mattresses. They agreed, afterwards, it was good was Goo-Goos: the most super feeling they'd ever had.

"My littles gets hard—like a crayon."

"Show me."

"Can't—it's gawn now."

"James, you *liar*, you."

His mother, he remembered, would kiss them goodnight and then, from the door, just before she turned out the light, would say: "Put your hands under your pillows now, like good children, say your prayers and go to sleep."

She must have found out something? But why hands under pillows? Was there another way? Anyway, Goo-goos was wicked, probably the most wicked thing you could do. He was pretty sure of that because he had such wicked thoughts when he did it and he did it every night. It was also bad for you, made you weak. It was a wonder there was anything left of him at all after all these years.

God he felt sick and he wanted to "go grunts" so badly that, in spasms, it took all his strength to keep from going in his pants. The Cure, he was bound to end up getting it. What was it? He didn't dare ask lest the mention of it cause him to get it.

He remembered another cure. It was that horrid English nanny they'd had. He didn't know how old he was but he was pretty little. The first night she'd given them both a bath and then she'd become very interested in his "penis" as she called it. Then she sat him on the toilet, told him to keep still and

38

grabbing the tip with the fingers of one hand she pulled the skin back with the fingers of the other.

"It's all wrong," she said with the same cold tone he was to hear so often. "The fosskin is stuck." She pulled so hard that he screamed. He screamed for his mother who he *knew* would stop this—he screamed very loud. She pulled until he was bleeding.

His mother burst into the bathroom. But to his surprise, after a lot of talk, his mother accepted the Nanny's view. No one listened to his pleas at all.

"Dear, dear, dearie me," his mother said. "How could I have known that the skin was supposed to go all the way back? Why my two elder boys were—you know, different— they had it snipped away just after they were born. That's why I didn't know."

"If the condition isn't rem'died it will lead to serious trouble and infection as he gets older."

His sister cowered in the corner by the dirty clothes hamper. Tears, pleading, screams of murder were to no avail. It was agreed that Nanny would pull the skin back a little each night until he was "fixed".

Every night he had to go through the same torture. "There, there," Nanny said to his protests, "I'm doing it for your own good. You know that. Still now, keep still. Steady . . ."

One night it hurt so much that he brought his clenched fists down on her head. She turned him over and beat his bare behind with a slipper.

James roared with pain and anger: fury at this total loss of dignity.

Did his sister come to his aid? He wasn't sure. But he remembered the Nanny said if they didn't behave she'd give them both something much worse than a spanking.

Shortly after that the Nanny had been "sacked". He couldn't remember why but it must have been his sister. His mother always believed what *she* said.

39

"It's no good, Jamie," she'd say sadly shaking her head. "How can I believe you when you're always telling such fibs? I know you want to be a good boy—so *please* stop. I've told you about the Boy Who Cried Wolf. And that's what you are becoming—the Boy Who Cried Wolf."

Trouble was, she was right. He *was* always telling lies. He couldn't stop. Why? Why do I do it? But there wasn't any answer. When his mother had first read them that story he'd cried: couldn't anybody feel sorry for the Boy Who Cried Wolf?

Even his sister, who he considered his friend, twin and wife (they had been married, after all, by their elder brother Teddy—Christopher had even consented to give away the bride) wasn't any comfort. "It's no good, Jam-Jam," she said shaking her head so that her pig-tails flew in a perfect horizontal arc, "if you don't stop lying you'll go to H-E-double L. Hell." The damn smartie, she knew he couldn't spell very well but he could spell that.

But as he lay there he thought of home as heaven. His radio was there still beside his bed; he had had to leave it. The radio really had been heaven: he tried to forget how he'd begged, whined and wheedled to get it. Playing his mother off against his father and his father against his mother. He absolutely *had* to have a radio.

Amos 'n' Andy were one of his favourites. They were so *stupid* and he'd laugh and laugh and for the whole length of their programme he didn't think of anything but them; it was paradise. They were nice people, Amos 'n' Andy. They couldn't help being stupid; after all they were only coloured.

Best of all was Jack Benny. "Rawawchester" was great, always being caught out the way *he* was. Mary and Jack were fine too; they did a lot of kidding but they really liked each other, you could tell. Then there was Inner Sanctum; he always went next door to his aunt's house to listen to it. It was forbidden at home but his aunt was American and she never told on kids.

She didn't have any children of her own and she wasn't good because she wore lipstick and smoked: Lucky Strikes in a beautiful green and black and gold package. She loaned him mystery books too; they had lovely bright covers with cellophane stuck on. He borrowed a different one every week and never read a word. They were forbidden too: he did it just so his aunt would like him. She'd have a whisky and soda and he'd have a coke (also forbidden) and they'd sit there like old cronies and listen to the spooky Inner Sanctum door squeak.

His aunt, they said, had once been very beautiful—"and now look at her". She just sat and drank whisky all day long. She was only twenty-five, they said, and just look at her. Well she *was* pretty flabby-looking but twenty-five was pretty old; he couldn't imagine himself living that long.

"Gaard's-sake, don't tell your mother," she'd drawl and then give him a book. "Hide it." Funny thing was he had what his mother called "a sneaking suspicion" that his aunt *knew* he didn't read the books. What's more, he thought, she knew that he knew that she knew—and if you kept on thinking like that, as he often did, you could get dizzy. Maybe he was wrong but he liked her, he couldn't help himself.

He didn't hide the books when he got home and he never asked himself why. His mother never noticed and he didn't ask himself why either. He knew his father wouldn't notice; he never even came into his room unless he was very sick.

He liked George Burns and Gracie Allen; Gracie was even more stupid than Andy. Fred Allen was funny too; you could laugh at his voice even when he wasn't even *trying* to be funny.

Recently the radio had talked more and more about those murdering and torturing little yellow Japs. He shivered and pulled the blanket up over his ear. Everyone knew they weren't really human and nobody would be safe until they were all dead. They'd make you eat pounds of dry rice and then force you to drink a gallon of water and the rice swelled and your stomach burst open. They used women and babies for bayonet practice.

One Jap had come into a woman's house—a pregnant woman—and he'd made her lift up her bathrobe and then he'd slit her stomach from between her legs upwards. The baby fell out, plop, on the floor. This story horrified him. But there was something else—?—Yes, it fascinated and excited him too. He must be the worst person on earth. Why was he so evil? He tried and *tried* to be good but evil just kept rushing in . . . was anyone else in the world like that? He didn't think so.

"That awful whats 'is name Crosby—can't even sing in tune," his mother said. He didn't mind. He liked the singing; he even liked Frank Sinatra ("A guttersnipe", his mother said, "saw a picture of him—looks like a piece of chewed-up string.") because when he was singing you could listen to the words and imagine yourself saying these things to a girl. Sweet words that swept you into sweet daydreams. Love, touch, darling, love, lips, dear, caress.

"They're either too young or too old," a girl sang. "What's good is in the army, what's left will never harm me."

"Doesn't even make sense," his mother said. It made sense to James—"harm". He knew what the songwriter meant and that was just what he'd like to do to a girl. "Screw" her, that was one of the words. "Fuck" her. Forbidden, exciting, ugly words made rapturously, soothingly, fiercely beautiful. Best of all here was a girl singing that she *wanted* it, even *liked* it. He wished he knew a girl who liked it, wanted it, *wanted him* . . . but that would never happen . . . they liked big boys of seventeen and eighteen and he'd never be that old . . .

The songs were *all* about sex and that was why he liked them. Even The Yanks Are Coming was sexy if you thought about it.

Jane Rogers. The memory of her made him wince and

blush: he'd made such a fool of himself. Jane was fourteen—impossibly much too old for him—an English girl evacuated from London. But he always dreamed of older girls: full and rounded ones—what good were flat little girls of his age? Jane had big breasts already. She and Charlie and he played marbles together. He was on the outside because Charlie was big: developed too and you could tell Jane knew it. As for himself . . . well, Jane's breasts were about eye level to him. He didn't quite know what he wanted to do with those breasts, just be around, near them, he guessed; all he knew for sure was that their delicious, vibrating, magnetic presence certainly ruined his marble game.

Charlie was as bold as he was shy. "You're my girl," Charlie was always saying—right out like that. Jane would blush and giggle. It became a competition to see who could be the naughtiest.

James's final contribution (how could he have been so stupid? he cursed himself) had been a note, in code, he'd secretly passed to Jane.

The code had been, he recalled, wishing now, even as he had done at the moment of the first exposure, that he could "kill himself", so simple and stupid that she had broken it in one day and deciphered his even stupider, babyish, silly message . . .

He had simply written backwards. "A kiss a day keeps the doctor away." "Yawa rotcod eht speek yad a ssik . . ." Ssik! Worse, in a rash of childish bad judgement, thinking she would not decipher it, he'd told Charlie that Jane (how could he have been so *stupid*; just because she'd blushed and smiled that smile when he gave her the note?) was his, James's, girl.

Charlie went straight from school to Jane's house. When James got there he hadn't even understood the meaning of their smiles and winks until Jane sprung the trap.

"Come here, James," she said crooking her finger, "I understand you want to kiss me. I dare you to—come on."

43

" __ __ __ "

What should he do, run?

"You see, baby James. You're too big for your boots. And what's all this about you spreading it all over Bermuda that I'm your girl? Eh? A twelve-year-old brat like you."

He turned and ran.

Their laughter rang in his ears even now.

As if to prove them right he'd cried like a baby when he got home. He would have squealed to some grown-up about Charlie being a bugger in the marsh: but Charlie could squeal too and then he'd really have to kill himself. His sister found him. He told her a watered-down and somewhat fictionalized version of what had happened.

"Those *stinkers*," she said stamping her foot. "Don't you worry, Jamie—just don't go *near* them again." She whirled her pigtails. "Ah me, the pain, the pain of unrequited love." Those crazy boo-boos sticking out like little tents.

And he couldn't tell anyone that he longed for Jane so much that just thinking of her made him feel sick—and wasn't it right after that that he nearly died of Dengue Fever? No.

But what was it he was thinking about before? There was something he had to remember. That awful nanny? No, they'd been so little then—something later. But was it that nanny who'd told them about birds and bees? He couldn't remember. Some nanny had said ". . . and then the daddy bird puts a seed in the mummy bird's tummy . . ." He'd thought of his mother and father, suppressed it with disgust and then imagined himself grown-up with a grown-up girl: pushing water-melon seeds through her navel. It had been exciting once, what a baby he must have been.

Gunpowder, that was it. Gunpowder and Jew-baiting and he and Charlie going on the rampage breaking windows, street lights, tearing down signs . . . "no, not horses Charlie, it's not right to frighten horses, dumb animals . . ."

And then all those really cruel and evil things he had

44

imagined doing to girls . . . no, he didn't want to think about it . . .

"WAKEY, WAKEY, RISE AND SHINE."

James woke-up, again thought he was at home and was again cast down; cast down, he thought, like Jacob when his brothers cast him into the pit. If he could only get back to Bermuda: even if he had to stay in church *all* the time he'd agree. Church was the lousiest place on earth—no, the dentist's was. But if he could get back to Bermuda he'd even agree to stay in the dentist's chair . . .

"Shut-up, you R.N. brownhatter. Where the fuck do you think you are, in a Wrennery?"

"Wakey, wakey, rise and shine, you've 'ad your time and I've 'ad mine. Drop your cocks and grab your socks."

It was 4.00 a.m., eight bells again.

"'Ere, you matelot bastard, pipe down."

"Yes, mate," Harry, "if Oi catch you in the tiller flat Oi'll show you the diff' between cocks and socks."

"You couldn't darling-dear—I've gotta left 'and thread."

"Ah get stuffed."

"You mean *you'd* like to. All you merchant navy blokes are the same—just like my ole man said—fuckin' poofters the lot of you. P*oo*fters."

When James next woke up he saw McIntyre coming down the steel ladder. It was 8.00 a.m.

"Bowsum-warns-ya, Faunteroy."

"What?"

"You 'eard you lord's bastard."

James had heard and, repeating the sounds over and over, he realized that McIntyre had said that the bosun wanted him.

"Where is he?" James started to put his coat on.

"Where the 'ell do you think?"

45

His face and neck hurt where he had been sleeping on his life-jacket. "Come on, I don't know."

"Aw, fuck it—'e's stuffin' his mug."

"I'm sorry—but I don't understand . . ."

"Eatin'—don't you know *nuffin'*? "

In the head he found he couldn't pee. It was the rolling of the ship, he thought. He held onto the pipe above the toilet and prayed. If anyone comes in I'll pull the lever and go out. At last it came. Surprisingly little. He ought to go next door and wash and clean his teeth but he felt too sick and weak.

On deck the damp and cold breeze off the dark water made him feel a little better. The horizon rose and fell but he had better equilibrium up here where he could see it. He started forward rolling like a drunken man. He remembered the drunken man he'd seen pee right on the sidewalk outside the Princess Hotel. It had shocked and embarrassed him. An Englishman, one of the censors, a gentleman just like the kind old one that tutored him in Latin. He'd never paid attention to his tutor—try as he might he just couldn't concentrate. He couldn't concentrate in school either: however hard he tried his mind just kept wandering off every which way. Why? Why?

But there was the man with this great big very white and very limp thing hanging out peeing in the road like a horse. James had stood quite still and pretended not to look but lots of people were openly staring. Another man, he remembered the exact words, came along and said, "Now, now, old chap. Will you be so kind as to let me see you home? " I wouldn't have helped him, James thought, I couldn't have—people might think I'd done it, and he pedalled off on his bicycle as fast as he could.

Little flights of spray came over the gunwale wetting the deck in patches making harsh black patterns. The purring of the vents and the small whining of the wind seemed ominous, the shipboard smells unfriendly and everything was so totally the antithesis, as his mother would say, of home that it reminded him of it constantly. It was, he thought, like someone playing music much too loud right up against your ear.

Stepping through the oblong loophole cut into one of the steel plates that divided the deck into sections, James almost banged into the bosun coming the other way.

"You wanted me, sir?" He was surprised at his own voice: he should have let Chambers speak first the way Grandfather said you did to royalty.

"Yes. I did. 'Ere, look, don't call me sir, see. You can call me Late-For-Dinner but don't call me sir. Well, 'ow are you feeling today?"

"Much better thank you."

"Well, I want to see you eat a good breakfast—nothing worse than an empty stomach. Come on."

"Do we have a good berth, Mr. Chambers?" Anything to stall—the thought of food . . .

"Eh? Yeah, not too bad. See that bloke up there?" Chambers pointed forward where, slightly abeam of them, the *Charybdis* stood out black against the white of her own spray and the field of white-capped waves between them. "Well, that's the Royal Navy, mate—it's better to see them than be blind I-can-tell-ya. Trouble is we won't 'ave 'em for long—two days and we get the bleedin' Canooks—or maybe the Yanks, God-'elp-us. But if we get to 'Alifax all right there's a good chance we'll be in a big convoy—bigger you are the better see . . .

"You don't eh? Well, stands-t'-reason, lad. If there's a lot of you the brass has gotta take care of you—lots of escorts. If there's just a few of you—well you're just not worth the candle, that's all."

"How do you know we're going to Halifax?"

"Just guessing," the bosun winked, "but we aren't pointing towards sunny 'Avana I-can-tell-ya. Come on."

The galley was stifling hot and the smell of cooking made his stomach writhe.

47

"Whatcha?" Cookie said, stirring a pot. Sweat poured off him and fell onto the stove making spitting sounds.

Harry Smith was leaning against the bulkhead sipping from a big white mug and smoking. "This lousy ship—not even a decent package of fags on 'er. Lucky Strike, sucky-like and lickey-dickey and it's all the same to me, George."

"Cookie, 'ow about some eggs and bacey for Lord Faunteroy. 'E ain't as beautiful as the lady upstairs but we've got to get some nourishment in 'im."

"No, I couldn't . . ."

Cookie smiled his two-toothed smile.

"Don't blame ya," said Harry blowing smoke straight upwards, his lower lip pursed in disgust. "Do ya know what Cookie's last job was? Feedin' pigs in Cardiff—'e's the reason why the 'ole crew's had the screamers ever since we left Baltimore."

"Now, now," said Chambers, "stop that. All right Berkeley, 'ow about just eggs?"

James shook his head.

"Well, toast and cocoa then—you 'ave to 'ave something."

James ducked for the steel door, stumbled out and made it to the ship's rail.

In no time Chambers was beside him. "The dry 'eaves, eh?"

James nodded.

"The Cure's the only thing for the dry 'eaves—but it takes guts. 'Ave you got enough guts to try it, nipper?"

He nodded.

Chambers led him back into the galley.

James suspected it was a trick but there was nothing he could do about it even if it was. He determined to go through with it without flinching; that would be best.

Chambers sat James down on a garbage can and stood over him. "Now, Cookie, 'and us the brew. That's it. Now, Berkeley, drink this. Come on. Right down. I'm not letting you up until it's all down."

48

He handed James a big mug. James drank some. It was, he thought, warm salt water.

"Just close your eyes and drink it right down."

James closed his eyes and drank.

"You'll never be sick again."

"Never no more—" Harry.

"When I first went to sea they made me swallow a piece of —"

"—not *after* this." Harry.

"—pork tied around a string and then I drank the brew. Crumbs I ran for the side and the string pulls the pork up—"

"'Eard that one before."

"True too. ALL-OF-IT Berkeley."

"Coo—you must've coughed your ring up." Cookie, tittering.

James finished the last gulp and then struggled blindly for the door. He vomited over it, opened it, vomited across the deck, skidded, fell and ended up prostrate, vomiting overboard through the small gap cut in the steel railing apron at deck level.

He vomited until he thought he'd go blind. Stars flashed. His head ached as if someone was driving nails upwards into his forehead just above his eyes.

He gasped for air and vomited again.

Then Chambers was standing over him. "You'll be all right now, chum. You're a sailor now. That's the same cure they gave old King George when 'e went to sea."

James tried to kick him.

"Stop that. I mean it. Tomorrow you'll thank me. Come on, back in your sack now."

"'Ere, I'll take 'im." Harry.

"If you tasted hairs, you're all finished," Cookie said in his high lilting strangely toothy accent. "'Cept, I 'spect you don't 'ave any hairs yet—*marvellous*."

It took James a long moment to understand what he meant:

49

hairs in your stomach? Then he understood and retched again.

"Can you make it to your bunk now, Faunty?" Harry, warm and kind, he really cared, at least, it sounded as if he did.

He nodded.

Together the Bosun and Harry half steered, half carried him down into the crew's quarters. When they got to the bottom bunk of James's tier Harry gave the occupant a kick.

"Get out-of-it, Mac."

"Fuck off."

"Hit the deck, McIntyre," Chambers shouted. "Come on, jump to."

—Chambers is really tough, thank God he's on your side— now. But watch out.—

"You can fucking scapa."

James felt himself lowered into a sitting position.

"McIntyre," Chambers boomed, "you ever talk to me like that again and I'll 'ave you up before the First Officer. You can 'ave Berkeley's bunk. Come on, 'op to it. Get your stuff up there and 'is down 'ere."

James tried to protest—it would mean trouble later—but he was too weak.

"And if you bruise even one banana, I'll-'ave-you."

Laughter.

"Yeh," someone shouted, "we don't want nothing to 'appen to them bananas."

James felt hands untie his life-jacket and pull off his shoes and then he was being bundled into blankets. The attention was the more comforting for its roughness.

"You really won't be sick," Harry said, bending down and patting him on the shoulder, "it really works, I promise ya."

"No, he won't," said the Bosun gruffly, "otherwise we'll 'ave to give him the Cure again. Understand me lad?"

Keeping his eyes tight closed, James nodded.

*

His Grandfather would pat him on the head. "Benjamin," he'd say in a deep affectionate tone, "our last-born, sold into Egypt." It was the same tone he used when he patted a dog or a horse but he used a higher one for cats and a higher one still for canaries, bluebirds and redbirds.

Grandfather was always saying things that didn't make sense. He wasn't the last born, for heaven's sake, little George was six years younger. But Grandfather was kind and he walked all the way over to their house every night and read them a bedtime story: or rather, he used to when they were small. Grandfather had a gold watch that you could see your face in. Grandfather smelled of a mixture of Angostura bitters and lavender (come to think of it, his father did too) and he always wore dark blue ties with little white spots and in his portrait he wore a white wig and didn't look like Grampy at all. "Dreadful thing," Granny said, "makes him look positively negroid."

Grandfather's name was Eugenius which meant Well-Born and that was fitting, James thought—but Benjamin?

"There, that's who you are named after," Grandfather pointed to the entry in the family Bible. He pointed with his little finger which had a small gold ring on it. Grandfather's hands had brown spots on them but they were very beautiful and he moved them very gracefully.

The entry was in ink and said "Benjamin Somers, left Bermuda 17th of March 1806 for New York. Heard no more of him." The last five words were written with a perilous slant "to starboard" Grandfather always said.

"There were other Benjamins too—Durrells and Halcyons as well as Somers. But that's the one I always think of."

In his bunk James drew his knees up until they touched his chin. Benjamin Somers had been a bad egg like him and had run away from home: that was what he'd always thought. Now he understood: Lost at sea, lost at sea.

The screw said, drown-ded, drown-ded. It went on and on

51

and he couldn't stop it. Drown-ded, drown-ded, drown-ded . . .

Think of something else quick. Anything. Grandfather. Trouble with Grandfather was that he'd only pay attention to you for a very short while. Then he'd start talking to Grandmother and you might as well not be there. Christopher too—when Christopher was home Grandfather didn't notice you at all.

But Grandfather, even Grandfather had noticed the day he stole the money out of the envelope, the housekeeping money that his father had given him to take home. Even Grandfather finally noticed there was something wrong with him.

It hadn't happened long ago—before the rampage and before his parents went on their visit to New York and he'd made the Fieldings's, who came to live at Westhill and take care of them, life a misery—and he could remember it vividly. It had been his last theft. He shivered with self-revulsion to remember that he'd stolen from his mother *three* times. How could anyone be so *vile*?

Why had he done it? It wasn't any good, as an excuse, to say that that year they forgot his birthday: forgetting was just a sin of omission and stealing was far worse. Besides, as his mother had said, she was so busy and there were so many children . . .

He had woken up in the morning very excited. His birthday! He looked about: no presents anywhere. He patted the bed where they were usually left—nothing.

It must be a surprise picnic, he thought, a lunch picnic with friends. But lunch time came and went. An afternoon surprise picnic . . . and he hung about all the long afternoon and then he *knew* it was an evening party with fireworks and presents. Nothing.

Tears. She promised a party the next week. She was sorry. "You never forgot *anyone else's* birthday . . . you . . . you . . ."

But stealing money: why had he done it? The only reason seemed to be that he wanted the money.

His father had given him the envelope at his office in

Hamilton. It was a small brown pay envelope with his father's name on it and the figure £17-19-6. For a whole family, a small enough amount: "I don't know how I can make ends meet," his mother was always saying. "We never had *any* money when we were first married and George kept his pay envelope. When I asked him it was just gone and he didn't know where. Fortunately even *he* had enough sense to agree that thereafter he'd bring it home—straight home every week and give it to me."

But his mother didn't know what *he* knew, and that was that his father cheated: his father had his secretary give him a separate envelope each week with a five pound note in it. It was awful to think of your father being a cheat. *Five whole pounds* and his mother only had a little more than three times that for the whole family. "Why I'm wearing *his* mother's *cast-off* underwear," she'd say. "The other day Daisy asked me for a cheque for the Tennis Club—when I told her I'd never had a bank account in my life she couldn't believe it."

"I pay all the utilities and God knows what else," his father said. But he betted they weren't much.

But £17-19-6. "Take it home to your mother, son." The envelope was very heavy. He jangled it. The whole 9/6 must be in change. He didn't want the £17-10-0 in notes: even if he could've bought every stamp he wanted for his collection. (He'd figured out often enough before that ten pounds would buy *every* stamp he wanted: ten pounds was The King amount of money.) But you'd never explain such an enormous purchase, you'd be caught for sure: besides, what would the family do? Anyway 9/6 was the same as nineteen weeks' allowance; 9/6 was a lot of money even if he had stolen, two times before, a whole pound note.

This time you couldn't explain a pound note but if the change was jangled enough on the way home the 9/6 would fall into his pocket. What then, super-crook, think? Then he'd have to hand it over. But if, say, there was a little hole

53

in his pocket the change would roll out. Right, not too big a hole so that the envelope would stay. A little hole and then he'd hide the 9/6 and tell his mother he lost it.

All the way home on his bike he jangled the envelope, in his pocket, up and down. But it just wouldn't develop a hole. He got all the way to their driveway and no hole.

He stopped and taking out the envelope he gave a mighty shake. The three heavy half-crowns and the two shillings flew out and clattered on the road.

No one heard. He looked all around. No one. He gathered up the change and shoved it into a hole in a cedar stump. Then he looked at the envelope. The corner of the red ten shilling note was peeping out. He pulled that out too and stuffed it in the stump. Wow!—To explain *that* would really test his mettle. Phew-ee!

Then he pulled one of the pockets of his shorts inside out. Pretty tough stuff. He rubbed and rubbed but no hole came. He cut it with his penknife. Then he continued up the drive: just like they said, "sweating like a stuck pig".

His mother and grandfather were having tea on the western terrace overlooking the water. The silver tea service sparkled in the sun; Grandfather's Panama hat was low over his eyes to keep out the glare. Although James twisted his face into the most tortured grimace he could manage they didn't notice.

They greeted him and then went on talking.

When his mother offered him tea he said, "I couldn't possibly eat a thing."

"His father's stomach," she said off-handedly and went back to their conversation.

He threw himself down into one of the teak garden chairs—nothing. He groaned—nothing. He got up and paced up and down like sea-captains in the movies. Wow, The Sea Wolf, Edward G. Robinson, it made him scared just to think of it.

Finally Grandfather said, "Gad, Charity, gad if I don't think something's bothering that young fella."

"What is it James?"

"Aw—nothing." Don't tell right away. To make it look good let her drag it out of you.

"Oh, he's all right," she said.

He had to start all over. This time when she finally asked him, he managed tears, produced the envelope, turned out the pocket and blurted out the story.

"My heavens," she said. "Look. Nineteen and six. I don't know how we'll manage. Why that's a whole week's wages for Matilda."

"I'll pay you back out of my allowance," he said managing a pretty effective wail. They'd never punish him for *that* long.

"My dear James, I swear you're as much trouble as the *whole rest of them put together*. Did you go back and look for it?"

"Yes. I've searched and searched. It's no good . . . I've been back twice . . ."

"Well then, run along. Go and wash your face—it's filthy."

He went away feeling strangely disappointed, empty, let down. He didn't know why.

Later, he remembered, he'd bought a wallet. The stamp shop was closed and he looked around the other shops. There wasn't really anything he wanted and so he bought the wallet. It would be a pretty noticeable thing; it would be hard to explain away, but he bought it. He even took it straight to his father's office and asked his father to write in the little card that slipped in behind the celluloid window. He did this, he thought, because his father did such perfect printing; terrible handwriting but perfect printing.

"Just print my name and address please."

"All right, Sea-egg," his father took out his tortoise-shell Waterman's, held it straight and carefully wound the bottom. The nib rose up; it looked almost alive, like a tortoise's head coming out of its shell. Like a penis. *Stop* that. "Where'd you get it?"

55

James shrugged. "In a shop."

"What on earth do you want a wallet for?"

"Oh, I dunno." He shrugged again. "Can I have ninepence to go to the movies."

"You went last week."

"But it's a good movie."

"What is it?"

"A funny one—Laurel and Hardy," he lied.

"Oh, I suppose so. Here, but for goodness sake don't tell your mother." (When his father said "your mother" it always sounded as if he meant "she's yours not mine", and that usually gave him a headache too.)

He went to a movie feeling emptier even than before. He forgot it in the movie but remembered it as soon as he was out in the sunlight again.

He rode home feeling utterly wretched. For several days he left the wallet around but nobody said anything.

Lying in the bunk he wondered what his mother would have done if she'd found out? He was too old for a spanking.

It was an awful long time ago but he could remember with a sharp and dark bitterness what it was like to be spanked by your mother. It was the worst thing in the world; when you were hurt you ran to your mother for comfort, there was no thought of anyone else. The world just became one big need —for *your* mother. But when *she* hurt you who could you run to? He used to bang his head on the floor. Once he'd tried to cut his wrist with the curved fruit knife in the pantry but he wasn't brave enough.

Last summer she hit him across the face with her clenched fist. It was his fault. His mother and father had had an argument that he had purposely fanned. When they were screaming at each other he'd called his mother "a bloody bitch". She'd slugged him, he deserved it.

He'd expected his father to tell him that he must never speak to his mother that way again. Instead his father defended him and even accompanied him down to the stable to feed the pony: something he'd never done before.

"Damnit, Sea-egg," his father said as they walked along in the half-darkness. "Damn if we don't get treated like a couple of *dogs* in that house."

James expected to feel happy and he pretended to. But he felt utterly miserable—no, he felt both happy and miserable. Why couldn't one feel just plain happy? he never did anymore; he could hardly remember when he had. "Thanks, Dad, I thought she was going to kill me." He was a Judas Iscariot, that's what he was. There was one in every generation and he was it.

KLAH-KLAH-KLAH-KLAH-KLAH . . .

"Action Stations, Action Stations."

It seemed as if the room was exploding.

"Action Stations, Action Stations."

"Christ-all-bloody-moighty!"

KLAH-KLAH-KLAH-KLAH-KLAH . . .

"God," somebody wailed, "Oh God, help us."

III

KLAH-KLAH-KLAH-KLAH...

James sat up, threw off the blankets and grabbed his life-jacket. The alarm bell rang on and on; it reached inside you echoing your terror. Or was it the terror of the bell, the ship, that he echoed? He didn't know.

The tapes of the jacket were still wet with his vomit. Maybe he should put his shoes on first—no, the jacket.

Men coming down from the bunks above bumped into him, stepped on his feet. Looking up he could see others already climbing the companionway.

"Come on, scapa."

"'Old it."

"Get-up-them-stairs."

His shoelaces hadn't been undone and now, in his haste he knotted them even worse.

"Stay in your bunk, nipper." Harry. "It's only a practice—or maybe a false alarm."

"No. I must get out."

"Holy-Mother-Of-God," a voice said, "and us not a day out. Come on, Harry."

"Can't wait, mate. Just put your boots on and stay in your bunk."

"Please wait for me," but Harry was gone.

58

James struggled with the laces. Never, never again would he not have them all ready. Never, never would he even take off his life-jacket.

Just as he got his shoes on the alarm bell stopped. The silence was intense, eerie. He was alone. It occurred to him that here was his chance to go to the bathroom without anyone seeing him. No one would come below now.

But say they were hit by a torpedo? What a price to pay: to be drowned just for one lousy . . . But he needed one so badly and it might be a long time before he got another chance.

"Eh, boy, where are you?" It was Cookie his head peering down around the water-tight door. "Look-it," he lilted, "you're to stay where y'are, Chambers says. So's he knows where to find you."

James ran up the companionway. "No, I want to be outside."

"Well you should'na."

"I must."

"Well, then, stay close to the hatch now—but don't say I said so. Remember I told you to stay in your bunk, mind."

Outside James wedged himself, facing forward, against the hatch cover. He was sitting right on the deck. It was steel and cold and he longed for a wood deck: wood was warm—friendly. Above him he could see men manning the Oerlikons and above them the upper decks and above them the grey sky with little puffs of black smoke coming from the funnel.

Then he heard the woman's laughter again. He looked up and there she was on the boat-deck holding onto the rail. Under her life jacket she had on the blue raincoat; her head was in a little scarf and every now and again she'd put her hand up to it. He wished he was with her.

Then she was pointing astern and a man came up to her and she touched her hand to her head again: such a soft womanly gesture. And then she laughed again as if it was all a joke, a game, and he saw there were two men with her; the other had always been there half hidden by a stanchion.

Shipboard smells: rotten oranges, cold tea leaves, stale stew; oil and garbage, always the same.

He jumped up to see what she was pointing at.

"All passengers assemble in the dining saloon." Peh-tuck. "All passengers assemble in the dining saloon." Peh-tuck.

Should he go? No. If he was well he was supposed to be at the locker opposite the Number 3 boat on the port side. And then astern he saw the plane. A biplane, sea-plane body, round engine shape between wings. Vicker-Submarine Walrus. He recognized it instantly. From the Dockyard, from Bermuda, from home. Oh, to be on board it.

Maybe the plane had caused the alarm? Or maybe they'd radioed for the plane's help: but then someone had said they were on radio silence.

He heard two heavy blasts of a ship's whistle. The Commodore ship. The blasts sounded like the baying of a sick animal.

BRRRAWAWNK—BRAWAWNK.

Like cows having calves at home. Home. Home and his mother saying they were going through the same *hell* women did. Guilt, sickly guilt. All men bad.

Then their ship was turning, you could feel it. Turning to port. The *Empire United* heeled, not into the turn as his father's boat always did, but outwards, to starboard, in a seemingly perilous lurch.

He looked up again but the girl had gone and the two men with her. Could he go to the dining saloon? No, he didn't belong there and he'd get into trouble. But it would be wonderful to sit up there in the warm. Maybe the woman would smile at him like she did on the tender.

There was a great and rapidly increasing staccato roar. There, passing to port, no higher than the ship, was the Walrus. So close you could see the square panes of glass that covered

60

the cockpit. There, a hand waving, fingers upward; such an offhand confident wave. He wished he was a pilot; pilots were the most super grown-ups. A pilot was the best thing anyone could be. Then he felt bereaved and bitter: *they* would be home tonight.

The plane banked a little and, as it passed by, the full force of her exhausts barked at them. It sounded, he thought, the way a German engine would: harsh, rasping, not unlike a machine-gun.

He watched the Walrus fly over the Commodore ship and then sweep forward in a long arc. He watched as she got smaller . . . two seagulls in the grey.

Teddy said the Walrus was a great old plane. The only one in the world that could land and take-off on land, the water or an aircraft-carrier. Teddy was in England taking his exams to gain Special Entry into the Fleet Air Arm. Christopher was there too flying in the R.A.F.; he'd written home a riddle about his plane so that they would know what he was flying: what is a bird with tapered wings, is a Spartan who died in the year 395 B.C. and is still found in the British Grenadiers?

Lysander, a crumby reconnaisance plane that couldn't even do 100 m.p.h. He told his friends at school that Chris was flying a Boulton Paul Defiant. Why didn't he ever tell the truth? Trouble was he was such a good liar: an amateur would have said a Spitfire.

Maybe Chris would meet him? But how could he, since no one knew exactly when he'd get there? No one even knew what port. No one, except God, knew if they would ever get there.

Then the alarm was over and what were, to James, the real problems facing him returned. How to keep from throwing up —his throat and mouth were too raw to take anymore—and how to manage a bowel movement without being seen.

He went and lay in his bunk and tried to pretend he wasn't there. I don't exist at all, he said, it's all in my imagination.

I'm at home dreaming and if I reach out I can turn on the radio and hear Jack Benny and Rawchester.

In the afternoon McIntyre brought him some cocoa and toast.

"'Ere, Cookie sent this."

"I don't think I can eat anything, thank you."

"Well you damn well better 'ad. I'm not your nursemaid—I'm an engine room peggy. Not my place to go runnin' around the ship waitin' on you."

"I'm sorry. I'll try and eat it." He sat up on his elbow and took the plate and cup. "And, look, I didn't mean to take your bunk."

"The fuck you didn't."

"I mean it. I'll give it back to you—really I will—as soon as I feel better."

"Come-off-it! And get me in dutch with Jerry piss-pot Chambers?"

"No—I'll tell him. I'll tell him I like it up there. I will—I do too."

"You're a tricky bastard. I'm on to you, don'choo think *I'm* not." McIntyre walked away. When he reached the bottom of the companionway he looked around briefly then shook his long hair back off his face, tilted his head heavenwards and clattered up the steel steps. The Sea Wolf—with pimples.

James tried the cocoa. It was very sweet. The seaman who'd dumped the garbage shuffled past. He looked at James, made a face as if he'd smelled something bad, "Coo." He smacked his lips once like someone calling a horse. "Coo."

The toast was thick and heavy with strange-tasting butter. He managed to eat a half a piece and drank about a third of the cocoa. Then he had to lie down flat again. "Ho-hum. Ta-tum."

It was true: if you kept quite still you did feel better. If you wedged yourself up against the ship's side you didn't feel the roll so badly.

62

Under the blanket he put his hands into his groin and closed his legs tightly; everything felt better that way.

He fell asleep and when he woke up it was night again. Eight o'clock and the watch was changing. The men were dressing, undressing, talking, laughing; he envied their acceptance of it all. They knew what they were doing, knew what would happen next; they were used to it. They knew each other.

"Christ, in't it awful not 'aving the radio no more," Hammersmith said scratching his head the way a dog scratches fleas. His hair was long and oily-looking like McIntyre's but McIntyre's was black and Hammersmith's a dirty yellow.

"Yus-mate, a bit-a-music don't 'alf cheer you up. But I didn't cotten to them Yankee crooners meself."

"Nah, I meant Vera Lynn. Coo, I love 'er singin'—turns me proper soff."

"You mean 'ard," a seaman said, going by with a towel and shaving gear. "Lyin' there flubbin-ya-dub. It'll turn ya balmy —I'm warning ya."

"No need to be *filthy*," Hammersmith protested, "the dirty minds some people 'ave. Well, I never—I was talking about music—*singing*."

When things quieted down James took the remains of the cocoa and toast to the head, dumped them in a toilet, flushed it, stole a pee, flushed it again. He was about to try for more but Hammersmith came in.

Their eyes met but, to James's relief, Hammersmith looked neither hostile nor friendly and he didn't speak.

He put the mug and plate in his locker; he'd take them back tomorrow, he thought.

"'Ere, Faunty."

James jumped. It was Harry and Paddy—"Harry's china" he'd heard. A china was a friend but somehow it seemed to be more than a friend; he didn't know quite how. Everything was more everything at sea.

"Brought you some pop. Yankee pop—maybe it'll remind you of 'ome. And 'ere's some chocolate too."

Pepsi-Cola and a Hershey bar.

James swallowed—gulped.

"Jaysus," said Paddy.

"Doncha want it, nipper?"

"Oh yes. Thank you very much. But—but, can I pay you back?"

"Naw—forget it. I knocked-it-off."

"—?"

"Jaysus."

"But my father said to always pay my way."

"Faunty, I *pinched* it."

"Oh . . . thank you." God! Stealing . . .

"Naw, mate. It's nuffin'. This ship is crawlin' with Yankee crap. Pepsi, 'Ershey bars, Lucky Strikes—the lot."

Paddy sat down. "I liked the Coke the best. In the States that is—but they don't 'ev any 'ere. Pepsi's too rotten sweet for me." His expression didn't change; it never did but his eyes seemed, somehow, to laugh. "Give us a fag." He snapped his fingers. Harry pulled out a package and flipped it at Paddy without even looking. Without looking either Paddy, his elbow on the table, opened his hand and when he closed it the package was there. He flipped a cigarette into his mouth, threw the package back and then snapped his fingers again. Harry produced some matches and the process was repeated.

They smoked.

"Mick bastard, got nuffin of 'is own except bad 'abits and a dose of crabs."

"Jaysus."

"Harry?" James asked, "Was that a submarine today?"

"Coo. 'Oo can tell? Could be. Luck of this ship . . ." he paused, looked at James, and turned his mouth down. "Prob'ly a false alarm. Go on, eat up. You'll feel better."

"Just a little. I'll save the Pepsi for later."

"You don't 'ave to eat it at all." Harry sounded hurt.

"No, no, I like it. I just have to be careful."

"Right, right. Save your strength. Tomorra Chambers'll loikly give you summat to do. Keep you busy like."

"What?"

"Taking stock of long and short weights—stuff like that."

Someone laughed. It was a seaman wearing a blue turtleneck sweater and a brown wool cap. He sat down and without a word took out a deck of cards and began shuffling them.

"What was you blokes steering today?" Harry asked.

"You know better than to ask that," the sailor said.

"Well then, I'll tell you." Harry took out a book. It looked like a school atlas.

"I just do me job—I don't ask questions. The man tells me a number and I turn the crank that's all."

"You could tell us."

"Hell I can. Anyway—today I didn't even listen."

"Whoi?"

"Spent the 'ole day playin' with little flags if you must know—"

"Well yesterday, accordin' to my figurin' it was 'Alifax. Today, I can't quite understand."

"'Ow do you figure?"

"The log's 'anging over the stern for all to see—then there's the after binnacle."

"But the binnacle's locked. 'Ow do you get in?"

"Girl locks 'er legs, mate, what-do-ya-do?—press the button, mate."

"Well, it's a fine lot of good it'll do ya with us steering a zig-zag course."

"I can figure that—fifteen degrees to port then fifteen to starboard, twenty minutes each way."

"Figure hell, you 'aven't even got it right."

"Yes-I-'ave."

"Harry can navigate, you know," said Paddy. "He's a proper mathematic."

"And my proper name," said the seaman, "is Alva-de-dell—'Oi read the news for the B.B.C."

"Why do we zig-zag—is it submarines?"

"Yus-mate. Supposed to be. Time they line us up, take aim—time it takes the torpedo to reach us—and oops, we're off in another direction. Works like a charm—'cept when it doesn't."

"Fucking Jerry torpedoes 'ave got eyes," said the seaman. "For all I know there's little men in them."

"Nah-nah, mind-your-manners."

"How soon will we get to Halifax, Harry?"

"Bugger-off to sleep now, Lord Faunteroy," said Harry scratching his groin. "You ask more questions than my ole woman."

"Your old woman—a pig's arse," Paddy said, his face remaining its normal gloomy mask.

"Well, I 'ad one once."

"A pig's arse, you did."

"You-can-say-that-again, Paddy-boy."

James lay there thinking, remembering something that had happened one Sunday afternoon at Westhill. It had surprised, shocked and bewildered him. It was during the time when he followed his father everywhere. "Like a shadow," "sticks to him like glue," people said. "That boy's the spitting image of him."

His mother and the others had been away somewhere and he and his father and his father's secretary were cleaning out the big mahogany cupboards in his father's study. The cupboards had all sorts of fascinating things in them: old postcards, photographs, war souvenirs, endless files of papers, letters done up in red ribbon, old potties, a lace Christening gown and a sword from the Boxer Rebellion. There was a box

66

he'd opened; his father took it away. "A-hum," he'd said. In it he had seen a glass thing shaped like a trumpet with a rubber bulb on the end.

"For electric batteries," his father said. "It's no good any more."

"Well let's hope you won't have any more electric batteries, then," Miss Snead said and laughed.

His father looked angry.

James had gone off to the bathroom. He didn't know what the rubber and glass thing was for but it was something to do with sex: it always was when adults tried to cover up. He didn't like Miss Snead, she was common and uppity just as his mother said. It was right that his father try to cover up— it was decent. And it was very wrong of Miss Snead to make some half-concealed crack.

They didn't hear him come back.

Miss Snead was up on the step ladder reaching into the upper shelf. "Oh Lordie," she giggled.

"What?"

"I've got a ruddy itch."

"I'll scratch it for you." To James's horror, his father shoved his hand right up Miss Snead's skirt.

She giggled again and then she saw James.

"_____"

"Eh—t."

Silence.

"Come on, old man, we'll make some tea."

It all proved, he thought, that his father was bad too. He didn't want to believe it. He hadn't, he thought, thought of it until now.

He shielded his eyes from the bright caged lights with the blanket.

It was all so wrong because once, long ago, his sister had told him an impossible thing.

"He *did*, I tell you. I saw him. He pinched her—right on

the bosom and then he pinched her coo." (A word they'd
learned from the Portuguese gardener: bottom.)

"You're lying. Mummy wouldn't let him."

"I don't lie. It's you who lies and *you know it*. You know
what's worse—she laughed. Isn't that awful?"

It was worse than awful. It was even worse than the time
when they'd seen their father threaten their mother with a
chair leg. It was long before he entered their fights, long before.
There were screams and they had run next door to get Uncle
Joe, Mother's brother. But Uncle Joe had only laughed.

"He's going to kill our Mummy."

"Well, I can't help it—it's none of my business." He
chuckled again. "Can't come between husband and wife. It'll
be all right, don't worry."

They appealed to their aunt but she just rattled her scotch
and soda and took a big drag on her Lucky Strike. "But you
sure are welcome to stay here until things calm down," she
said.

"Well if he kills her," his sister said and stamped her foot
in front of Uncle Joe, "it will be *your* fault."

Men were cruel, that was all. Often he'd heard his mother
say, when she was tired: "Men! Oh God help women. Angels
help women. There's no pain on earth like the pain of child-
birth. No man, *ever*, has experienced such pain. And I've been
through it five times."

Which meant they'd *done it* at least five times. Then he
remembered with embarrassment and anger: fury, the story
they were often telling *on him* to other adults. He'd heard them.

"James—he's a scream. One Sunday lunch—he must have
been about five—there was a silence in the conversation into
which James suddenly and solemnly announced: 'Mummy,
I've discovered that you and Daddy have done something
perfectly disgusting at least five times!'"

Roars of laughter. Well, so okay, they'd done it ten times,
a hundred times: as if he bloody well cared.

"It's not Mummy" he told his sister. "She doesn't like it—she *couldn't*."

"No. *He* makes her do it."

But that was long ago. Recently he hadn't been able to talk to her about such things. Once, thinking it would please her, he'd said, pointing to her little breasts, "Well, they're coming on—getting bigger and bigger every day." She screamed, slammed her door and locked it. Bawled her head off.

His mother sent him to his room in Coventry, for the rest of the day. "You can stay there until your father comes home. God knows I've done all I can—*he* can deal with you now. I wash my hands of you."

No manner of wailing, persuasion or sweet talk could get around her that day.

"And I hope he thrashes you so that you won't be able to sit down for a week."

It had been a long day. He was, he thought, a changed man by the time his father got home. Fortunately his father wasn't angry at all, just very quiet. All he said was, "You can't say those things to women, old man. They don't like it. You understand?"

And every night he went back into his private world. The world of goo-goos. The golden fantasies more remote than fluffy clouds, more real than technicolour movies; a vibrating re-creating of a world, of himself. A world in which he was both the victor and the vanquished; a world over which he was master. Ah, sweet flight of rose-petal numbness, sweet peace even greater than the peace he knew when they gave him morphia when he broke his tibia and fibia. "Ah, for this I'd break them twice a day and three times on Sunday."

To be alone and enter his private world. The longer dragged out the better and who better than he, the world's greatest liar, to spin and spin the web of joy...oh land of milk and honey.

He was a schoolmaster. He was the all-powerful school-

69

master. The pupils male and female, sometimes the one, sometimes the other, sometimes both or neither: it didn't really matter.

The schoolmaster had the pupil in his study. "You've been bad. You've been very bad. Haven't you?" The longer drawn-out the better. "Come on. Say you've been bad."

"I've been bad."

"That's it. Say that you've been very bad."

"____"

"Come on. Say it or you'll get a spanking now as well as later."

Whimper. "I've been very bad."

"Well then, what do we do to little people who've been very bad? Come on, you know."

"I don't know."

"Come on, say it." Pinch.

Flinch. His own body flinches. Sweet flinch. Sweet whimper.

"Say it."

"You spank them."

"Yes we do. That's just what we do. So now, just take down your pants. That's it." Pinch. Flinch. Sweet bare touch . . .

"Yes. A nice little bottom. It will do very nicely." Whimper. Wriggle. "But you've been so bad this time—so utterly wicked that I've something special for you. Can you guess what it is?"

Draw it out. Oh sweet long flight. Draw it out.

"Well, you've been too too wicked this time. I'm afraid it will have to be something worse than a spanking."

"Oh, no, no, no. *Please*, no."

"Shut up or I'll give you something to cry about."

"No, no."

Wriggle.

"Oh, yes, yes. Pull your pants up, now." Oh, save that bare sweet treasure touch for later. Later, later—again.

"Can you guess what it will be?" The tormenting, all-powerful tones of schoolmasters, nannies—*demons*.

"No. No."

"Ah yes. A spanking in front of the whole school."

"No. Oh, please, no!" Flinch and press, sweet spasm-press. Wriggle.

"And what's more you will have to have it on your *bare* bottom. Bare, stripped, your bottom showing to the whole school."

"No, no." The whine. Whine and squeal.

"Ah, it will hurt me more than it hurts you. After all, it's your fault. You've been impossibly wicked. There's no other hope for you."

The headmaster makes a long speech to the whole school— ah, draw it out—with the victim standing there.

And then the sweet commands. "Take down your pants. Still now. There, there," caressing voice. Soothing voice: to take the victim by surprise.

Crack. Sweet flinch and press.

Screams. He himself utters a small sound.

"Stop that now. If you cry, I'll have to use the cane. *You heard me*—all right. Head-boy, bring me *the cane*."

"No, no. Anything. Please, anything but the cane."

"Still, now. Absolutely still."

Crack!

Flinch.

Pause.

Crack!

Flinch.

Pause, pause, pause.

Crack! and then Crack-Crack!

"There, you weren't expecting that were you. Ahah—ha."

Crack! Flinch. He himself squeals now. The live sound excites infinitely; uniting real world and his world, making his world totally real. The heavenly sweet and tormenting rise into satisfaction.

Crack, flinch, crack, flinch, crack, flinch . . . rub, squeal, flinch. Aaaaaaa—Aaaaaaah. The moment of total rapture: the five ticked spasms of milk and honey. The sixth tick—pause, rising to the sweet and almost painful precipice of the SEV-ENTH!

Only to return, hot, heavy, gasping, sweating into the harsh and tormenting reality of one's little and defenceless life. The first long moments of abject fear lest one was heard. The longer moments of guilt; the self-devouring knowledge that one houses within oneself a monster-self that is one's true self, that will, inevitably either devour the little self or else be found out, discovered by all-powerful adulthood—or both.

Oh God, help me!

No, no, pray God God didn't see me.

But God sees everything. God is everywhere. You will pay in hell. You will go to hell and PAY, PAY, PAY. The store of your sins is stacked high. Two hundred nights. A thousand. You are the most evil person that ever existed.

She had said so. No, she didn't really ever say so; it just felt as if she had.

Charlie was evil, a sinner too; but Charlie was not like this. Charlie was just sexy—which was evil enough—but he wasn't cruel about it. He didn't dream of torturing people. Charlie was sexy but kind about it; you could tell the way he was afraid of hurting that time in the marsh. No one must ever find out. You couldn't even tell a guy like Charlie about these secret vicious things . . .

Heck, you couldn't tell Charlie anything any more.

And yes, there wasn't any sense in hoping, praying, the fantasies would go away; they didn't, they hadn't, they only got worse. He prayed to God to help him; he'd prayed with all his might. But God did not help him: and why should He? Why should God help a disgusting little boy like him?

The schoolmaster was put away; to be used sometimes, for a change, but less and less frequently. The secret world became himself as a grown man and the girl with the bursting big breasts in the tight blouse bound to the chair with her hands tied behind her.

The writhing upon the bed and he the man advancing upon the girl; Jane Rogers, yes, but more beautiful, more mature and *frightened*, her nipples sticking out like little frail, but hard, buds. And the man, not caring, enjoying her frightened look, advances and pinches one nipple hard. She squeals, writhes with pain but also with pleasure; a delight she tries to hide but he knows about. "You think you can fool The Whistler, bitch!"

And he playing first man then woman, pinches, writhes, squirms and squeals. Becoming both at the same time. Double joy.

The bonds are loosened but the hands still bound and he strips off her blouse (slipping out of his pyjama top) and caresses, caresses the fat round firm breasts: then, 'of a sudden, catching her unawares, pinches again and again.

Squeals.

He turns her around and starts to strip her of her skirt.

"Scream all you like. No one can hear you down here in the dungeon."

And then she is in her frail lace pants and he fingers all about her private secret parts.

"Do you know what you are going to get?"

"____"

"Answer me bitch."

"No, please, no."

"Yes, yes—and if you don't do it and like it I'll take this cane—see it?"

"No, God, no, please."

"And I'll whip you until you can't sit down for a week."

"Help, no, no."

"Shut up. If you don't shut up I'll bend you over and shove the cane right up your bottom. Ugh."

"Aaaahaha . . ."

"Christ-Almighty, Faunty. What's up? You 'aving a night-mare?"

"Blooming night-'orse if you ask me. A night-charger."

"Fuckin' arse'oles, pipe down!"

He pulled the blanket over his head. The life-jacket cut into his back. He turned towards the ship's side, bit his thumb, and tried to hold back his tears.

It's my own fault, he thought, I'm being punished. I haven't even said my prayers since I came on board. But surely, God, you can't expect me to get on my knees here?

You would do it, God said, you would if you weren't a coward.

I am not crying. I AM NOT. I've just caught cold on deck. A likely story. Tears ran down from one eye, across his nose and into the other. He kept silent and hoped no one would notice the shaking.

The next day James woke up wondering why he felt so good. Something was wrong with the world but what was it?

Smells of men's sweat and the strange metallic painty odour of shipboard; the sounds of throbbing machinery ...

Yes, it was hell but there was something better about hell ... ? The ship was hardly rolling, that was it, and, to his surprise, he didn't feel nearly as seasick as before.

Moving carefully lest the nausea return he went and washed his face and cleaned his teeth. At home they always made a noise to accompany teeth cleaning. "Nee-ee-ee-ee ..." He didn't know why, they just always had. There were two other men in the washroom and he was careful not to make the noise.

Peeing was now less of a problem. If you were careful to watch and enter the head when no one was in it, then you could induce it by flushing and then it didn't matter if someone came in. Once you were started there was no stopping. Someone see-ing his penis, seeing him peeing, was a worry but it was nothing, for some reason, in comparison to taking down his pants.

74

On deck he felt the ship rolling gently in the ocean swell. There was hardly a ripple on the deep royal-blue water; just the rising and falling of unfurrowed hillocks. The sea looked so unfathomably deep, yet so impenetrable to the eye. You couldn't see down into it an inch never mind the twenty odd feet you could see down to the bottom in Bermuda.

How deep was it? A mile? Five miles? He shuddered.

Gu-rung. Gu-rung. Gu-rung.

The ship ploughed her white wake: a mark so vast, but, he knew, so soon to be swallowed up by the sea. The sea could swallow up the world and not leave a trace.

He was on the starboard side. He felt the sun warm on his hands and face. He felt very grateful for it. Funny how this was the sunny side now. What had Harry meant, "sunny side going home"?

Braw-awnk. Braw-awnk. Braw-awnk.

The Commodore ship's horn was not quite so frightening in daylight.

Two officers passed pacing the deck.

"You wouldn't credit it for February, would you now." An old man with white hair showing under his peaked cap.

"More like June. Can't last, I suppose, sir." A tall young man who looked quickly at James and then quickly away as if he hadn't meant to notice him at all.

The ship yawed in her turn to starboard.

"... Horse Latitudes ... dust-up ..."

Sound of the younger man laughing very enthusiastically.

James decided to walk right around the deck before he tried to eat. He'd walk a few yards and then stop and look over the side.

Swee-eesh. Swee-eesh, went the giant hull as it rose and fell throbbing ever forward.

Forward, where there was a gap in the rail and a steel ladder leading down onto the fore-deck, he paused. A seaman was tapping the wedges on a cargo hatch cover with a big mallet.

75

Funny you couldn't hear the sound. Then, turning one ear towards the man, he heard the sound wafted up on a changing breath of wind. He watched the hammer fall: sight, pause, clunk. It was eerie; the man might be a ghost risen out of the water. He turned away and started over to the port side.

What was wrong. *Charybdis*. That was it. H.M.S. *Charybdis* was gone. He ran to the port rail. Their sister ship was there and beyond and slightly astern of her the tanker, long and low in the water. Funny looking ship a tanker; all the works astern: funnel, engine, crew's quarters, everything. That was because, he knew, the oil (it might even be petrol) was forward and oil could catch fire or blow-up. But no *Charybdis*. No escort anywhere.

For two days James did his best to "learn the ropes".

"I don't expect much from you right off," Chambers had said. "Just report to Cookie when you feel up to it."

"Lord's bastards always get all the breaks," McIntyre grumbled and spat into a garbage can.

The mess and the adjoining galley were the hardest places to keep from being sick. Each time when first he entered he was glad of the warm but soon afterwards he was too hot. The constant smell of cooking was nauseating even though he took to breathing through his mouth—a technique which helped considerably. One of the worst smells was exhaled smoke. The men smoked heavily, they seemed to swallow the smoke down into their stomachs and when it came out the smell was acrid, poisonous. He noticed it was especially bad when the men had just got up from sleeping and were getting ready to go on watch; he learned to keep away from them as much as possible but it wasn't always easy.

The food was strange: bully beef and yellowish cabbage that smelled like seaweed and mashed potatoes swimming in greasy gravy. The men liked "bread and dripping" too; dripping was hardened bacon fat and there were cans of it left out all the time on the two long tables. One of his jobs was to keep them full.

"Dripping 'ere," Cookie would shout each time he cooked bacon and James had to find the emptiest can and take it over. "Watch your 'ands, now." James tried to hold his breath through the whole operation.

Sometimes he mixed powdered milk with water in great pots; at others he washed dishes and scrubbed pots. Scrubbing dirty pots made the vomit rise in his mouth but he would swallow it back, close his eyes, pray and then take deep breaths. But he was an extra hand and most of the time he just sat around. Everybody sat around a lot. There was a lot of waiting in war, he decided. He'd take a box and sit right under the vent. The air here smelled heavily of machinery and oil, but it was better than the smell of cooking.

"Whyn't you take your coat off, you'll fry in 'ere."

James thought it best to keep it on.

One job he hated was taking "char" down into the engine room. He didn't often have to do it, it was McIntyre's job but when Cookie was off, Newsome, the man he'd first seen dumping garbage, sometimes made him do it.

Newsome never spoke except in muttered obscenities. He never walked, always shuffled. His face was gaunt, his eyes glazed and suspicious and he had the habit of raising one leg slightly and then breaking wind.

"T'engine room. Fuck-off," he'd say and push the heavy pot across the soiled brown linoleum counter top.

To get to the engine room one needed both hands to operate each of the two doors. This meant putting down the pot, opening the door, climbing through, reaching back for the pot, putting it down again, closing the door—twice.

Once in the engine room one had to negotiate two long tiers of ladder downwards. The pot was heavy, you really needed two hands: the steel ladders were steep, you really needed two hands for them too. The only way it could be done was

77

to make a noose of one's arms around the ladder with the pot in your hands.

The heat was almost overpowering; the noise assaulted one's bones, skull. The men seemed like creatures blackened in hell. When he spilled the char they yelled at him but he never understood quite what they said. He just smiled and nodded.

He felt, constantly, both the fear that he would fall into the churning giant machinery and a frantic claustrophobia: what possible chance would one have of getting out of this fiery cavern if a torpedo struck? The machines, the engines would go wild, break loose, fly to pieces and you would be boiled alive in escaping steam.

When he climbed out on deck he gasped with relief. How could they stand it down there? How would he ever go down again?

But the worst job was putting the blankets in the Number 3 Boat on the port side.

"I don't care what else you do," Chambers said, "but every time the alarm goes, you're to open this locker and throw those blankets into the lifeboat. That's what the Old Man wants and that's what 'e's going to get. You understand?"

The locker was not far from the boat and the blankets were tied with stout tapes so that they were easy to carry but all that protected you from the sea—far, far below—at the moment when each blanket had to be thrown upwards, was a four inch steel gunwale. There was no railing and nothing to stop you falling into the sea, if you slipped, except this small gunwale. The lifeboat was above and its slippery curved side offered nothing to grab hold of save its small steel keel, and by the time your hand reached that it would be too late and the next thing you would feel would be the sea. James knew he would never get used to it.

"All right," said the Bosun on the afternoon of their third day at sea, "you can go on regular watches now. You aren't seasick any more, are ya, lad?"

"No."

"Well, Cookie, when do you want 'im?"

"Don't matter."

"Port watch then, Berkeley."

"Are you on the port watch?" James asked Cookie when the Bosun had gone.

"No, we cooks 'ave our own timing." Cookie smiled showing his pale pink gums.

"How do I know which is the port watch?"

"Watch 'Arry and Paddy." Cookie's accent was even more difficult to understand than the others. Sometimes James had to repeat the sounds over, to himself, three or four times to get their meaning.

"This fuckin' ship is steering every which way," Harry said. "Four days out and I thought we'd be a coupla 'undred mile below 'Alifax. But the way I've got it figured 'ere, we're 'alf-way to the bleedin' Azorees."

James was only half listening, he was watching the door to the head. He still hadn't had a bowel movement and his lower abdomen felt as if it was filled with cement. Worse, the spasms now had become so intense that he knew he couldn't hold it much longer.

If he went in his pants he'd really be in trouble. Everyone would smell it. Then what would he do? Get some clean ones from his locker, go to the head, roll the dirty ones in a bundle and then throw them overboard; but then the time would be forced upon him. Someone was sure to be there. It was unthinkable.

Newsome came out. Here was his chance.

He walked slowly over and went in. No one.

Stink. God, to be thrown in among all these lower-class, rotten, filthy stinking oiks. Newsome. Stinking filth of a man.

He hurried to a bowl, tore down his trousers to his knees, wiggled the life-jacket up as much as he could and sat down.

79

The seat was still warm. Disgusting to sit where that dirty man had sat—one chance out of six. It was unfair. Maybe Newsome was diseased? It was too late to move.

Nothing would happen. He looked down at his still sun-burned knees, on which grew tiny bright yellow hairs, and his hands with the bitten nails. The sight of them increased his consciousness of his own frailty. In desperation he pressed and pressed. Then something enormous was happening. It hurt so much that sweat broke out on his face. It hurt so much he had to stop. It went away. He pressed again. He prayed to be home. He prayed for his mother.

It hurt so much he found himself doubled-up, leaning forward, groaning. God, no! Stop, stop, he told himself, someone might come in at any moment. Shut up and hurry, hurry.

It hurt until he felt nauseous again but he gritted his teeth and pressed; with a rush of fierce pain it happened. He was so relieved he forgot the pain for a moment. He pressed again; it hurt again. I'm going to die, he thought, right here.

But the pain lessened. It lessened each time. When he got up there was blood in the bowl. I'm bleeding inside, he thought, I'll bleed to death. But I won't tell anybody—I'd rather bleed to death than tell anybody. Mother . . .

In a fumbling hurry he wiped himself and flushed the bowl.

He pulled up his trousers. His bottom hurt, it hurt when he moved. He should wash his hands. Mummy!

Mum-mum-mum-mum.

He felt too weak. He went and lay down in his bunk.

He felt a little better with his blanket over him. He remembered having diarrhoea at home and how wonderful it was to get back into bed after sitting on a lavatory so long that you ached right up yourself and your legs had gone to sleep. Bed had been, then, a warm and soothing haven and he'd fall asleep. If he ever got home again—got to *any* home again— he'd never leave. NEVER.

*

"I want my bunk back like you said."

"Oh, come on. I don't feel well."

"I've squared it with Chambers. You're pretendin' anyway —you feel fine."

"No—I'll tell you what. Maybe there's something I can swap you."

"Like what?"

"I don't know."

"I suppose you want to give me them bananas?"

"No. They're not mine—but I've some things in my trunk."

"What fuckin' things and I don't see no trunk."

"It's in the hold. I've some ..." What did he have? Only clothes and—no, he couldn't give away his prize ...

"Naw, naw. The bananas or nothink."

"No. I have something ..."

"What do you 'ave?"

"Some boxing gloves."

"Go on. Real ones? Leather 'n' all?"

"Yes. The best. I won them."

"We 'ad gloves at the club—in Kentish Town—Lord's bastards owned it—" Hammersmith said.

"Shit-you-did. Little twirp loik you never done no boxin'. 'Ow am I going to get them anyway?"

"When we dock. I'll give them to you—I promise."

"—from a posh school they were. We 'ad a 'ole gym— charity-like—"

"I promise I will."

"—we used to bust it up regular every Christmas. Can't think whoi—feeling just come over us."

"What-do-you-tyke-me-for—a idiot. I don't want your bleeding old gloves anyway. Boxing gloves, blimey. You kill me, Faunt-el-roy, 'onestly you do."

"But I haven't anything else I don't think."

"What about your watch?"

"NO."

"Come on, you can get anuvver one—*you* could."

"Certainly not."

"You snot—you fuckin' snots are all the same."

"'Ow about some cash?" Hammersmith said. "'E's rich. I'll betcha 'e is. I 'eard 'im tell 'Arry 'is dad's a shipbuilder."

"Roight. You give me a fiver and you can 'ave the lousy bunk."

"No."

"Two quid, then—right? Less than 'alf."

"No. No money—I don't have any, anyway."

"Fuck 'e don't," said Hammersmith. "Let's rough 'im."

"Rough 'im, hell—let's fuck 'im."

"Knock-it-off. You know I don't like that—no dirt. Swearin' is one thing but dirtiness is summit else."

"I was only joshing, china."

"You can have the bunk," James got up. "And for your information the Purser has my money for me."

"Purser? Purser? Never 'eard of it."

That night, his fourth night at sea, he lay there thinking about life. He felt weighed down, burdened with the weight of what he knew about life. He felt burdened too with the fears of what he did not know.

He did not know what was in the future. He did not know what would happen tomorrow: even in the next hour, the next minute. To be blown-up? To be trapped here below, the ship sinking? To feel the cold water? To swim? To drown? To die? God, what was it like to die?

He did not know if he had one person on this ship who really cared what happened to him; he didn't really know if there was one person in the world who cared. Surely his mother and father? Surely his sister? Christopher? But what good were they now?

Perhaps if he thought about sex he could forget, forget about

82

the water. It was bad to think about sex but it was the only thing that worked.

It was quite likely, he thought, that he was the baddest, most dirty boy in the world: but sex *did* exist and it was very important. It was funny the way most adults pretended it wasn't—except coloured people . . .

Sex was a dark, a black secret and a big part of his life seemed to have been hiding from it, being caught by it and then hiding the whole thing, under pain of death, from adults.

Living in the world was all a matter of tricks and lies. Not the lies he told to impress people—and they were bad—but the lies one had to tell to survive. It was all wrong and he felt that it was, somehow, his fault.

Even in school there were lies. "When was America discovered, Berkeley?" America? North America or South America? Besides he knew that, in fact, it was not known when either was discovered; but the teacher had some date he had mentioned earlier and *that* was the answer that must be given. When an adult asked a question it was usually best to try and guess what answer they wanted. He had become quite good at it and that was *bad* too.

Once he had asked his arithmetic master a question he had been puzzling with for a long time. "Sir, I don't understand why two plus two—or even two multiplied by two—must always equal four? Because, I mean, no two twos are the same . . ."

He was punished. He had to write out a hundred times, "I am an ignorant little boy." The master said that the next time he was so smart-aleck he'd be beaten.

But he wasn't all that ignorant, he thought, because he knew quite a lot about coloured people and about sex. You didn't always have to tell lies to coloured people. Coloured people liked or disliked you (mostly liked) whether you told lies or not. Coloured people sometimes told the truth whether you liked it or not and they knew too that one must never tell the truth to adults.

At least, all this was true when you were little. As you got older they changed: he didn't know why. They seemed to smother you somehow. "Give them an inch and they'll take a mile", his father was always saying. "Never be familiar." His father was right. They were supposed to call him "Master James" but as soon as he was nice, he noticed, they called him James.

He had thought about it a lot and he remembered having a nightmare about a big sweaty Negro kissing his mother. The world was falling down.

You couldn't always trust coloured people but it wasn't their fault because they were somehow inferior. They were descended from slaves and, before that, they had been savages in Africa; dancing, killing and eating each other since the beginning of time.

But a lot of coloured people were nice too; they were generous and kind and he wished there was one on this ship.

He thought of Ruth his last nursemaid. Ruth was bad because she was sexy. But he had loved her because she lent him comic books and gave him gum; because, after the English nannies she was so soft and kind; because, in her way, she loved him.

He remembered one day he had gone into her room just before she left for her afternoon off. He was forbidden to go in there.

Dressed in a white slip, Ruth was cleaning her teeth, her strong brown arms flashing back and forth, her breasts shaking under the silk.

"Why are you always cleaning your teeth?" He yearned for something, he didn't dare think what. He felt bereaved, betrayed, homesick that she should leave him even for an afternoon. He remembered feeling angry too that she was adopting, aping, the ways of white people—the slip, the teeth cleaning. Weren't they supposed to chew bones or something? She would soon not be their Ruth, *his* Ruth.

84

"Because U'm gotta date. Any man's gonna put his tongue in Ruth's mouth gonna find it nice and fresh. Don't you clean your teeth when you gotta date?"

Tongues in mouths!? He was so disgusted he was excited; he was so excited he was disgusted.

He stammered. "I don't have dates. I'm only nine."

She gave him a knowing smile and laughed. "Your whistle is too small, huh? Well you keep on pulling him and he'll get bigger, huh?" He ran away. She was bad, wicked, disgusting: he should have told her off, cursed her. He was a coward but he couldn't say anything that might hurt her because then he might lose her.

He had gone off and pretended he was Superman jumping off the stone walls in the garden (if you just believed, believed hard enough, had *real* faith, you could fly; and sometimes, when he tried extra hard it did seem that his feet touched the ground a little more lightly . . .) and wrestling with invisible adversaries. Bop! Pow!

Shortly afterwards Ruth had been fired. She had been found with a Cuban in her room.

"I don't mind her having a little fun," his father said (which proved, again, that he was bad and sexy, but not, James hoped, as bad as he was) "but in our house—and a *white* man."

"It's all too disgusting," his mother said, "I don't want to hear another word."

His mother was often saying that the lower classes and the Negroes were all the same and not to be trusted. At other times she said they were just like children, "so lovable".

He tried to remember a time when he had been happy. Surely he hadn't always been wretched? If he could only think of a time when he had been happy it would be something to hang on to—to nurture and pull around him like a coat.

The sailboat, the *Longtail*! he had been happy that summer he had the sailboat all to himself. A man had loaned it to him.

85

He had never even known the man's name. It was a mystery: a mystery just like the mystery when he was a little boy and suddenly, one day, an enormous parcel arrived for him from out of the blue. They were in Bognor and it was a cold winter and the King was sick, people kept saying, and suddenly this beautiful package arrived. It contained the most super creation he'd ever seen: a Donald Duck and not a crumby English toy but big A. A. American. It was three feet high and the outside was all kid leather in the brightest colours: blue jacket and cap and dazzling white for the body and head and a screaming yellow for the beak and webbed feet. And it was perfect: exactly like Donald in the movie cartoons—and, most important, it was HIS, nobody else's.

Some crazy man, his mother said, had seen his photo, once, on the grand piano at Grandmother's house in Bermuda and simply said, in a crazy American accent that he "just *loved* that boy and hadda send him a present." Well he, James, just loved that man whoever he was. It was really cosy to think that someone loved you that much: he kept Donald Duck with him all the time and thought about the man who loved him a great deal. Gradually Donald had taken on life: Donald was his friend and Donald loved him.

And he had forgotten the man until the summer he was suddenly loaned the *Longtail* for two whole months. Was it the same man? His mother said no (she didn't even remember, at first, about Donald Duck), but, as he sailed alone in the little boat, he liked to think it was.

He had longed for a sailboat for so long. His father said no, they were too expensive. He'd tried to build one but it ended up looking like an oversize and busted orange crate and it didn't even float.

Then suddenly this beautiful boat: a glistening, sleek, mahogany clinker-built cat boat—almost new and with a spotless white sail: long, slender and graceful like the wing of the bird she was named for. And he was ten and he sailed her all day and every day from dawn until after sunset for two whole months.

Every morning, after breakfast, he took sandwiches and a bottle of water and he set off. He sailed every bright summer inch of Bermuda's azure harbours and inlets: he sailed out and all around the Great Sound and sometimes all the way to Somerset . . . He stopped and lunched on deserted islands where no man's foot had set before; sometimes he made voyages of discovery and sometimes he beached her on lonely sands and wandered looking for Friday's footprint—and he was always alone.

When there was no wind and the water a glossy, immaculate, virgin calm he would row her a while and then stop and listen to the water sounds that only accentuated the sweet silence: the drops falling from the raised oar blades, a fish suddenly breaking water, or the call of a kingfisher or a cahow from the umbrella-topped and spider-footed mangrove trees.

Sometimes he was one of his seafaring ancestors: Beau Nat Durrell, in his brigantine *Susanna*, sailing to the West Indies for salt, spices, molasses and rum; and then on to New York to trade and return home again to his beautiful wife . . . (Beau Nat, he knew, used to go on to Newfoundland for codfish . . . but to heck with that leg, he wasn't going to stink up his ship this trip.)

Sometimes he just lay back in the boat and put his feet up on the centreboard and thought thoughts that man had never thought before: since Grandfather said that nothing could be created or destroyed, only changed, then this must apply to sounds as well. Therefore, stone, especially hard stone, must have absorbed every sound that had ever occurred near it. Each stone was like a gramophone record: if you could just find a way to release the sound you could listen to all of history . . .

. . . what was beyond the stars? More stars. And suppose all the stars beyond the beyond were all contained in a single crumb on a giant's table and the stars above the giant the same —on and on forever. Scary, but, in the bright summer day, interesting. Suppose those crumbs, there on the *Longtail*'s cross-thwarts, each contain an entire world, stars and all? If you could go up forever, outwards into bigness you could go down forever, inwards into littleness . . .

Sometimes he whistled tunes he made up himself and sometimes he spoke poems, aloud, that came to him then and there—it was terrible stuff, so terrible that sometimes he broke it up with laughter . . . but, who cared, no one was there to hear or criticize . . . Blow thou sweet breeze and make the water lap and laugh me home . . .

He heard a woman screaming in agony.

KLAH-AH-AH . . .

No, it was the alarm bell—now only a few inches from his head—going off with a noise, his mother would have said, fit to waken the dead.

KLAH-KLAH . . . "ACTION STATIONS!"

He was out of his blanket and pulling on his shoes. God, his life-jacket, he should never have taken it off; but it was so uncomfortable you couldn't sleep.

The ship was rolling again now but he managed to pull on his overcoat kneeling in the bunk. Getting on the life-jacket he was alternately bumped against the ship's side and the opposing small guard-rail of the bunk.

"ACTION STATIONS! ACTION STATIONS!"

The bell clanged on: a cadence not unlike his own heart beat.

Looking up he saw two duffle-coated and blue bell-bottomed figures half up the companionway. The R.N. gunners. God they were fast—slick. No matter what the men said.

James jumped around and scampered down the vertical ladder. Half-way someone banged into him. It was the same as before: a mess, a tangle, you couldn't get out.

88

"Fuckin' arse'oles."

There was a jam-up on the companionway.

Intense whisper: "All right, nipper? Yeh, go on, you first."

"Move for Christ's sake."

"Night attack. Jerry must've gone crackers."

KLAH-KLAH-AH . . .

"There's a fucking moon, you cunt."

"S'only a false alarm."

"Jerry torpedoes 'ave got eyes."

Going up you had to be careful that the heels of the person in front of you didn't knock your teeth in.

They burst onto the deck like oats from a slit sack. The moon was out but it was very hard to see where you were putting your feet. Steel eyes and cleats seemed to keep catching at him. Men in front and men behind.

Up one ladder. Less men now. He caught a glimpse of McIntyre; followed him up another ladder. Boat deck. He scampered around to the port side, wrung down the two clamps and swung open the locker.

The ship gave a lurch. He grabbed the locker door, panting. When she continued her normal roll and pitch he grabbed the first blanket.

"Twenty-five blankets in each boat. That's what the Old Man wants and that's what he's going to . . ."

Peh-tuk. "All passengers assemble in the dining saloon."

Thank God the deck is dry. Legs apart. Swing. Swing up and over.

James's boat was the after one and McIntyre had the one forward of it. He could just make out his figure in the moonlit darkness.

"Three," James heard himself shout.

Pull. Walk. Stagger. Legs apart. Swing. Swing up and over. Again.

"The Capt'in's got a thing about fuckin' blankets," McIntyre had said. "'E was caught once in a boat without blankets—or

89

they was all wet or summit. Anyw'y, that's what we 'ave to do
—blankets, blankets, blankets, every time the old pell-mell
goes."

Swing up and over. Five.

"Stop trying to talk like a Londoner," Hammersmith was
always telling Mac. "You're a farmer—a Kentish farmboy."

James wished he was a farmboy right now.

Swing up—below the void, the sea—nine.

Swinging up the twenty-second blanket James's foot slipped
into the small incline of the gutter that bordered the gunwale.

He screamed as he fell. He lay spread-eagled on the slowly-
heaving deck, the wad of blanket under his chest. Below and
close-by was the chasm of darkness and below that the ocean.
He couldn't even see it. Swee-eesh. Chushsh. Swee-eesh.

He eased the blanket against the small gunwale and waited
for an inward roll of the ship.

Then he crawled back to the locker. He thought he must
have screamed very loudly, but then, when he caught his
breath, he realized he hadn't screamed loudly—he might not
have screamed at all—it had all been inward.

I could have gone clear over the side, he thought, and no one
would have known. I would have just let myself fall, silently.

He left the blanket, which had fallen with him onto the deck,
until last. He timed the roll of the ship and was very careful
where he put his feet. It was hard. It would be easier if he had
sneakers. The timing would be easier in broad daylight . . .

Twenty-four. He couldn't see McIntyre. The ship must have
turned; ahead the deck was now in shadowed darkness.

He reached for the last blanket, the blanket on the deck.
The ship gave an unexpected lurch. He was on his knees. He
let himself fall flat, reached for the blanket and then rolled
inwards again.

He lay there.

KLAH-KLAH-AH . . .

Why do they dare make so much damn noise? Radio

silence; not even allowed to *listen* to the radio and now this noise. Bells, bells all over the ship.

The ringing stopped. He felt as if he'd willed it.

He threw the last blanket into the lifeboat. Then he heard a clang, clang, behind him. The locker. He went over, closed it and then moved gingerly astern.

Here, just aft of his boat was a three-barred railing facing astern. He sat down, slipped his legs under the bottom rail and let them dangle. Whatever happened he had to wait. His arms were through the middle rail and thus wedged he felt a little safer.

The ship was quieter now. The wind was blowing from an angle behind them, stern-quarter, they called it.

He could hear the propeller pounding with muffled thumps; it sounded like Joe, the gardener, beating the rugs at home. Gah-vumb, gah-vumb, gah-vumb . . . The sound was absolutely the same: except Joe beat slower.

Only a few feet out and slightly below him was the round basin of an Oerlikon gun mounting. Here sat two men at their station. The presence of living people close by was precious to him; best of all, by a stroke of luck for which he was more grateful, he thought, than he had ever imagined he could be, one of them was Harry Smith. The other was an R.N. gunner.

He could hear them whispering. He wanted to call out but he didn't. He could see the horizon, all the way from the starboard quarter, around the stern and around to port until his vision was cut off by the stanchion that supported the strange modern davit slides for the lifeboat. Out there somewhere was the Commodore ship.

It felt good to be wedged. It felt good to see the horizon; the roll and pitch of the ship were understandable, not so threatening, when seen by the eye not merely felt in the stomach.

"See anythink?" Harry.

"Course not—'e'll see it first anyway."

91

James could just make out the duffle-coated arm pointing up to the look-out platform of the after mast.

"Christ, I'm glad I'm not up there. Muvva didn't raise me to be a steeple-jack."

The look-out platform, long and railed, made a perfect cross against the sky except that, above the platform, the mast emerged in two pieces, like two thick flag-poles one slightly shorter than the other. On one side of the platform, leaning out to port was the small figure of a man. As James watched he moved all the way over to the starboard side.

The long minutes of fear ticked by: it was not unlike crouching in the bushes playing kick-the-can with older boys... "That's good," he thought, "think of anything, remember something..."

James was just thinking that he was, hanging there through the rails, very like Teddy sitting on the cross-bar of their father's bicycle—back in the days when he and Vicky could both fit in the basket at the same time—when there was a large and heavy thud followed by a noise like someone falling downstairs.

"Oh, Jaysus," Paddy wailed. Where was Paddy? He couldn't see him. Waiting in the strangely vibrating silence he realized that the thud and rumble had come from across the water. He had seen a flash of light too. Perhaps it was only sheet-lightning?

"It isn't us anyway," said Harry. "Not yet it bleedin' isn't."

"Shut up..." The gunner's voice trailed off.

James could see them nervously turning the cranks that moved the gun's barrels back and forth and up and down. He checked the tapes on his life-jacket and let his fingers run over the smooth and rounded top of the light pinned to the left shoulder.

"This light goes on automatically when immersed in water ..." the tag said. He had read it over and over. The last time, he realized, was when he was sitting on the lavatory—head, toilet, w/c, shit-house.

Somebody had been hit with a torpedo. Not us. Not yet. He strained his ears—

Gah-vumb, gah-vumb, gah-vumb and the counter-point pounding of the engine and the purring of the vents and swish of the sea below. He looked down at his hands and saw that he was shivering: which was strange since he wasn't cold. Strange phooey, scared . . . but he wasn't really scared either . . .

"Look. Look at that," Harry, pointing out to sea. James turned. The Commodore ship blew her horn, two thick blasts like groans in the night.

BRAWNK—BRAWNK

"Not her either." Harry. "But look."

The *Empire United* made her turn to port: more steep, it seemed than before. Heeling. Heeling perilously.

Then James saw the tanker. There were no flames coming from her and no explosions but he knew she was hit. The whole scene, contrary to his expectations, was totally without drama. Upright, yet low in the water, the tanker looked like some dying animal.

He had expected great towering flames and thunderous explosions: but this ship just looked dead. She seemed to wallow there in the dark water like a hippo sinking into the mud in a Tarzan movie. Then black smoke started to ooze from her sides as if her guts were falling out.

Their course brought them even closer to her. She seemed quite still now in contrast to the rapid flow, bounce and surge of the sea passing by her . . .

Closer still . . .

So close it seemed they might bang into her, belly to belly.

James saw little figures running helter-skelter about her stern section. Amidships and in the bow all was still. Then she yawed away from them, or they from her.

"Good luck to you lads," someone shouted. It might have been Paddy. Of course they couldn't hear him; James could hardly hear him.

He watched the tanker fall astern. He strained his eyes and thought he saw waves breaking over her decks but he wasn't sure.

Foo-OOT—Foo-OOT—Foo-OOT.

"Destroyer," Harry said, "where the 'ell as 'e been 'iding?"

James looked all about; he couldn't see it. Now he couldn't see the tanker either.

"Must be a Yank." The gunner.

"The Yankee destroyers don't make that noise—it's British."

"A lot you know."

"Could be the *Charribus*."

"Shut up, will ya."

They waited a long time and then they heard distant deep explosions.

"Depth charges, eh?" Harry.

No one answered. They waited again. They waited a long time.

ALL CLEAR. ALL CLEAR.

To get the blankets back into the lockers he and McIntyre worked together. It was almost as frightening as the loading.

He had to climb the small ladder attached to the stanchion, hoist himself into the boat and then throw the blankets down one by one. He felt, all the time, that the boat might tip; or let go altogether and fall into the sea.

"Come on, 'urry up."

They finished his boat and he climbed down: the moment of leaving the lifeboat for the ladder was the most frightening. The sea seemed to be beckoning him; forcing him to look down. It was magnetic. He closed his eyes and swallowed; the swallow seemed to shudder all the way down to his

94

stomach and then left his legs weak. He forced himself to move.

They went for'ard.

"Up you go, then."

"It's your boat."

"No, no. Up you go—you're the unloader."

"I am *not*."

"Go on, or I'll *do* ya."

"It's your boat and your turn and I will not—"

McIntyre drew back his fist.

James stood his ground.

"Go—or I'll bust you."

James put one foot in front of the other in a boxing stance and put up his dukes. He was shaking; his legs felt like two used soda straws.

"You think Oi'm afraid of you."

"You think I'm afraid of you."

"I'll bash your fuckin' mug in."

"Possible but not probable," Christopher's phrase, "in either case, I won't get in your boat."

"You won't, eh? And what makes you think not?"

"The Bosun wouldn't allow it."

"'Ow'd 'e know?"

"What?"

"You'd tell him, I suppose."

"I will if I have to—I'll tell the Bosun."

"All roight—you wait. You just wait. I'm going to get you, Barkleee. You see if I don't. You fucking snot, you. You just wait and see."

McIntyre climbed up. He threw the blankets down. James stowed them. McIntyre climbed down and walked away.

James put his forehead against the cold steel of the bulkhead. He was still shaking with fear and rage. Then he burst into tears.

He cried for some time and then he decided that that was

95

precisely what he would do, he'd tell Jerry Chambers. If he didn't tell Chambers he'd tell Harry; he'd tell somebody. It was too dangerous not to.

But everything was dangerous. All McIntyre would have to do was give him one little push at the right moment and he would be overboard. McIntyre could do it too . . . Maybe he should stab McIntyre in the stomach with his penknife . . .

He stood for a moment on the after end of the boat deck and looked up at the main-mast. "Oh God," he prayed, "please let me live one year—just one more year *on land*, that's all I ask for. I know I don't deserve it—but *please*, just one year."

And the screw droned on:

M'MUM—M'MUM—M'MUM—M'MUM.

IV

James went down into the crew's quarters—fo'c'sle they
still called it despite its location—glad of the warmth and glad
of the company of the men.

SWEAT, SMOKE, PAINT—would the smell of paint never
go away?

There was a strange new atmosphere, a mood. He didn't
quite know what it was but it was something like being in a
thunderstorm: you wanted to run away but for some reason
stood stock still. A part of him wanted to be on deck free of
this feeling, free of smells, noise . . . but a greater part wanted
the company of humans. Scared, he realized, he'd rather have
any company, even McIntyre's, than be alone.

"Ain't it a bitch, eh."

"That destroyer—did anyone see 'er?"

"Oo says it was a destroyer?"

"Gotta be—that noise—and then the bangin', that was depth
charges, I'd know 'em anywhere." Harry.

"Well was it?—'ere Royal Navy, do ya reckon it was depth
charges."

"You're fuckin' aye, it was. And I 'ope they nailed the
bleeders—"

"Fuckin' night attacks—I ask-ya, wake me up outa me
sleep—Christ, and we go on watch again in five minutes."

97

"And I was dreamin of a bit o' skirt I met in Baltimore—sixteen, tits like little peaches—"

"Get off my fucking foot—"

"—'Er mother was lovely too—didn't look any older—"

"But this bleedin' ship. I tell ya—a bad 'un." Harry. "Oo ever 'eard of a ship being torpedoed way to fuck over 'ere by 'Alifax?"

"—What-a-life. I was stuffin' 'em both—send the daughter out to the movies—"

"Thought you said we was near the Azores?"

"—and into the sack with the mother. Other times, mother goes to—"

"Those poor bastards. Jaysus, did you see 'um running about like little ants . . ."

"—church and the daughter's got me on the carpet before the door's closed—"

"Well, shut up then—it'll be us next."

"What do you mean, 'way over 'ere by 'Alifax, Smith? You can be torpedoed any bleeding where these days. Why do you think New York, Baltimore and Philly is crawling with British seamen? Survivors, you idiot. Chroist, even Boston is full of us, they tell me."

"I know. I know."

"—No, the daughter would rather fuck than eat—"

"Anyway, where'd you and Paddy catch it?"

"—yeh, a blinkin' maniac. Lovely grub."

"I've been over three times and Paddy twice—"

"—the daughter's quimm 'ad real little blonde 'airs—"

"Well, it was off 'Ampton Roads—least that's where we fetched up. But we weren't torpedoed—"

"—that's what you call a *true* blonde—in'it?"

"What then?"

"A mine. Blew the bow right off."

"A mine, shit. 'Ow do you figure a mine?"

"'Merican mine—least, that's what they said. Stands to

98

reason, don'it. I mean, that close to America—Jerry wouldn't risk it."

"Chroist."

"No," said Paddy. "Harry's right. You know the night we copped it—well, earlier you could see the lights of America. Lit up the whole sky—orange and purple, very pretty it was."

"You can be torpedoed anywhere—didn't the skipper catch it off Trinidad?"

"Yeh, but that's sarth, in'it? Sarth you can expect anythink."

"Him and Chambers was on that Furness tub—old cruise ship, they tell me."

The place was a mess of discarded oil-skins, life-jackets, sweaters—a mess of men. When they were changing it seemed that he couldn't look anywhere without seeing a hairy armpit. STINK.

"And that bastard Billings was with 'em too."

"Careful, careful."

"I mean it—Billings is a proper bastard. One of these days that fucker's gonna stand too close to the rail—"

"Officers. I-shits-'em."

"What's up with Billings's foice, anyway?"

"Ecks-seema, I 'eard."

"Syphilis, more like."

"Syphilis, hell. Who'd ever fuck 'im?"

"Watch it! The walls 'ave ears."

"Come on, china, I'm for some java."

"Eh, McIntyre, weren't you on that ship with Chambers?"

"I certainly was. I was on a life raft with the Chief Engineer. Mr. McLeod—same one."

"Coo," said Harry. "I didn't figure you for a lad as learned 'ow to swim."

"'E can't."

"'E ain't as green as 'e is cabbage-looking," said Paddy.

99

"But a swim in the tropics is one thing and one in the North Atlantic another—not to mention the Denmark Strait."

"You can say that again, mate." Harry. "Yeah, Paddy, tell 'um about that little dip you 'ad in the Irish Sea."

"Irish Sea in't much," said Hammersmith.

"Cor—'ark at 'im. E'll find out."

"Naw. I mean it's near 'ome, though, in'it."

"That's where the Jerries really 'it ya, near 'ome. And the Irish Sea nipper—I'd as soon be dead—"

"Cor what's all this about?" Chambers came striding by. Chambers walked like a cowboy.

"Eh, bosun?" Harry. "Is it true this nipper McIntyre was with you when you bought-it off Trinidad?"

"Yeh, he was there. A picnic it was. Only in the boats a coupla hours. Bloody Jerry hit us within sight of land, you know. Cheeky blighter. They'd 'ave got us rescued sooner—only guess where we drifted?" He laughed. "Into a bleeding great minefield. Cor, what a lark." He lit a cigarette. "Well, what's with you 'Ammersmith, what are you lying there dripping about?"

"Nuffin'."

"What's the matter—miss your muvva?"

"The poor lad can't swim, most likely."

"Well, that's what your life-jacket's for, boy, keep it with you."

"I'm not the only one," said Hammersmith. "Mac carn't swim—and that Fauntelroy. I bet *'e carn't.*"

"I can so," said James. "I could swim before I was two. I can do a hundred yards in eighty seconds flat."

"You liar." Hammersmith.

"Nobody can swim that fast," Harry's R.N. gunner announced.

"Christ 'e can lie," said McIntyre, "'e told me 'e was a boxing champ. *'Im, a boxing champ!*"

"Give-over," Paddy spoke without even looking at James.

100

"Besides, maybe he is a champion—I'd bet he could handle you anyway."

Oh, God, no.

McIntyre was laughing.

"Pipedown," said Harry. "Was that a submarine, bosun?"

"Christ, Smith, you know damn well what it was."

"And the destroyer—was it a Yank?"

"Pray God it wasn't. More likely the Canooks—which is just as bad."

"But, the Canadians," said Hammersmith, "they're *British*—like, it's all the same, in'it?"

"Get some sea time in."

"You'll find out. Canooks, they're more like the cock-sucker navy than us."

"Cut out that filthy talk."

"Yes—it's proper disgusting," added Hammersmith.

"Nah, bosun. That's what everyone calls 'em—don't tell me you 'aven't 'eard it."

"Well, stow it, I said."

"It's all I ever 'eard from the Yanks," said the R.N. gunner. "You British cock-suckers this, you Limey cock-suckers that."

"I said *stow it*."

"All roight, all roight, but it's like they don't 'ave no other words. Funny bastards they are."

"You can say that again."

"Funny bastards they are."

"You can say that again."

"STOW IT."

James, still in his overcoat and life-jacket, sat on a locker. Things had quieted down and he was waiting for an opening to speak to Harry. He'd start, he thought, with Harry and maybe Chambers, who was writing a letter, would join in.

McIntyre had just left and as he went up the ladder he

flashed James two fingers—the signal for "up-you". Only the men usually said, "Up your arse," or "Up your pipe with a wire brush."

"Harry," he began, but his courage ebbed away at the sound of his own voice.

"What is it, cock?"

"Oh, I was just wondering about those men on the tanker."

"God-help-us," sighed Paddy, "the poor lads."

"But, I mean, the destroyer will pick them up, won't they?"

"Jaysus."

"Well, Faunty—you see ... well, in a convoy ... well, you can't stop. You stop, well, you're like a good target see. But somebody'll get them. Maybe the destroyer will, later. Or they'll wireless their position like—to another ship."

"But we're on radio silence."

"Yes, well—well, you never know, see. They've got all sorts of new fangled ways of signalling these days."

"I'll tell you what, lads," said Paddy, "let's all go for some tea and a nice smoke. Come on, Berkeley. Come along with us."

Chambers looked up from his letter. He had on glasses with flat lenses so that the light flashed on them. He looked quite different in glasses, almost like a schoolmaster. "Here, you two. Don't go giving the boy any smokes—you 'ear me?"

"All right, Jerry, all right."

"I mean it."

"It might make me sick, anyway," said James smiling.

"Yes," Chambers went back to his letter, "and you know what that would mean."

The three of them were alone at the galley table. Cookie was over stirring one of his pots; Hammersmith washing dishes.

"I don't quite con that bosun," said Paddy.

"Nar. You never know, do you?"

"He's been very nice to me," said James, man-to-man.

"Well, watch 'im," said Harry.

"I don't understand?"

"Well, mate, it don't pay to get too close see. 'E could turn on ya. I mean, like, it ain't like 'e was one of us, see."

"But I thought he was your friend."

"I ain't got no friends—save Paddy—not really. And you too if you like . . ."

"Oh, yes. Thank you . . ."

"Bosuns and quartermasters—peh!" said Paddy wrinkling his nose.

"—?"

"Can't trust 'em. See, they're apart, see. They don't even know whether they're officers or not—in a pinch, they'd turn on ya. Turn ya in."

"It's the truth," said Paddy, "drop of a hat they're coppers. Bunch of Guardo at heart."

"Yus, mate, you're better to stick with us—we'll watch out for ya."

"Officers and petty officers," said Paddy, "priests and coppers—sure 'n' they're all the same."

James was bewildered and frightened. He didn't want to take sides: especially where he hadn't known sides existed until now. He didn't want to lose their friendship but he couldn't afford to lose what little ties he had with Chambers either. Besides, Chambers was law and order, you could tell that. And what were Harry and Paddy up to? It made him very anxious. Whatever happens, he thought, I'm not getting into any trouble. Maybe they're after my money? That's probably it; they just want my money.

"Don't look so gloomy," said Harry. "'Ere, 'ave a fag."

"No. No, thank you."

Harry looked hurt—affronted, almost disgusted with him.

"You see . . . it's not that it would make me sick so much . . . well, I promised my . . . mother. I promised my mother I wouldn't."

"Faunty, you're a one, you are."

"No," said Paddy, "'tis right to keep your word to your mother."

"Yes," said Harry, "and you keep your word with us, too, eh? Don't you go telling Chambers nothing—roight?"

"Of course not."

"Nothing you see or 'ear?"

James shook his head.

"The worse thing you can be is what the Yanks call a stool-pigeon, roight?"

"Yes."

"The world's full of the bastards," said Paddy and he snapped his fingers, as usual, without looking at Harry, for a cigarette.

"Mick bastard. Got nuffin' but a lot of bad 'abits and a dose of crabs."

It was the morning of the fifth day. Where were they? Nobody knew. "This fuckin' ship is steering every which way," Harry kept saying and then he'd lick his stubby pencil and bend down over his notes and school atlas.

At eight bells they turned to. The destroyer was nowhere to be seen, only their sister ship now stationed ahead of them and seeming further away than before. Overhead, the sky was overcast and the sea a dark grey, flecked with whitecaps.

James went into the galley.

"There never was a destroyer," Cookie said and smiled. Nothing worried Cookie, he wasn't "all there".

"Either the Jerries got her too or she's scapaed and left us to our fate." McIntyre shook his head like an old man. He had black circles under his eyes; "must have liver trouble" his grandmother would have said. "Needs a dose of milk of magnesia."

Chambers burst in. "Take some char to those boys aft. I got them splicing cable and they're dripping bloody murder."

"Where did the destroyer go, do you reckon, Bosun?"

"What's the matter, you nervous?"

"ME? Course I'm not nervous."

"Then you've got less brains than I took you for."

Cookie shoved a pot and two mugs across the counter. "Aft
—and don' drop it, mind."

"Where are they?" James asked.

"Bosun's locker, you idiot," said McIntyre. "Don't you
know *nothing*?"

"Well, you take it then," Chambers said.

"But I'm off duty," McIntyre whined.

"My mistake, my mistake. After deck house, nipper. Hop
to."

The bosun's locker reminded James of the storeroom at his
father's boat works: it smelled of manilla rope, oakum, paint
and the not unpleasant odour of greased wire cable.

"Christ—it's only the nipper," said Harry. "You didn't 'alf
scare me."

"Jaysus," Paddy wiped his mouth with the back of his hand
and shoved something under a pile of cotton waste.

"Here, Chambers sent me with this."

"Tar—and-very-nice-too. The bastard—see what 'e's got us
doing now. Splicing wire! And Jerry all around us. If I thought
we 'ad any rights on this ship I'd slap in and see some basket
about 'im."

Harry was talking too fast.

"Yeh, 'e's got no 'eart. I spoke to the R.N. Chief again. 'E
said it wasn't *a* submarine it was *four* of the bastards. 'Ow
about that? Christ, we gotta live, 'aven't we."

James turned to go.

"Don't go, Faunty. Stay a while. They'll only make you do
summit else. You've got to learn to swing the lead a little."

"No. I must get back."

"Remember, sprog. What the eye don't see the 'eart don't
grieve for. Right?"

"I didn't see anything."

"Right-you-are then, chum."

"Do you think it really was four submarines?"

"Nah, don't let it worry you. Could 'ave been porpoises. Any rate, I reckon we'll be off 'Alifax shortly."

"Gee, I hope so. And then we'll have a big convoy, won't we? Escorts and everything?"

"More than likely. Don't worry, that's all, mate. Just keep your clothes and shoes on, see—and stay on deck as much as you can. That's my advice—for-friends-only. Anything 'appens, stick with us."

"Thank you. I will." It was all very confusing. He didn't really trust them any more. He wished he could be alone to think. McIntyre, that oik-rat McIntyre.

James finished his watch at noon. He went down to try to steal a quick bowel movement but the fo'c'sle was crowded. He went back on deck and sat, huddled in his great-coat, in his hiding place between the after deck house and the wooden raft. The raft was rigged, tilted, ready to drop into the sea.

"There, see," McIntyre had said to Hammersmith, "them two ropes. Same as on me last ship—the *Farrow Castle*—all you gotta do is cut them two ropes with that there axe." The axe was clamped to the bulkhead. Even the blade was painted grey.

"That's what I did. I let 'er go—saved our bacon too. But you 'ave to be careful." His voice took on the tone of a proud veteran. "Mustn't let 'er go too soon. Gotta wait till the ship's stopped moving—which is all too soon, I-can-tell-ya."

"Sh-sh. Look 'oo's listenin'," said Hammersmith.

"Yeh. 'Ere 'e is again. Always sucking around, eh Faunt-el-roy?"

Now, as he sat there, the wind caught at his cap. He pulled it down low on his forehead so that he had to tilt his head back to look out at the awful sea.

He felt, again, weighed down by what he knew. He tried not to think of anything but when you stopped doing things it was very hard.

It was hard, even, not to think about war. *The War*. The War was Hitler. Hitler was an evil man with a moustache, a loud voice, black riding boots and an arm raised rigid.

Hitler was a maniac but he was also CLEVER. England would win because England always won, they said, but secretly James didn't believe it. Hitler was an evil fiend and *because* he was evil, James thought, he would probably win ...

The Germans were awful people who bombed, blitz-krieged and made everybody homeless. Homeless. They killed men and boys and raped women and girls.

What, exactly, was rape? More than fucking. Grabbing them and giving it to them whether they like it or not—Yoweee!

Come on, he told himself, cut that out! God is watching, listening and your score is already ...

Sweesh—swoosh—sheesh ...

U-boats. Submarines. The Germans and those stinking sneaky U-boats. They torpedoed you and then they machine-gunned the bobbing heads on the oily water. They would have machine-gunned the tanker's men if it hadn't been for the other ships ... But the oil, the oil got into your lungs and choked you to death.

Why had the war happened anyway? The war had happened because there were some awful men who wanted to own every-thing: Hitler, Mussolini, Goebbels, Goering, Himmler and Tojo. They were all ugly, all horrible and all foreigners. They none of them believed in God—except the Japs, who were the worst, because they believed they *were* Gods when really they weren't even human.

The Japanese would beat the Americans easily because the Americans were all fat slobs who stayed out of wars lining their pockets with gold until the last minute and even when they came in they were cowards who boasted and waved flags and had a lot of brass bands and everybody had medals and practically nobody had heard a shot fired in anger.

The Statue of Liberty had a coke bottle in one hand and the other in her pocket fondling England's money and her back was turned to America anyway. (Although he knew his father said some of this just to annoy his mother who was part American—although she swore black and blue she wasn't.)

He drew his knees up and pulled the coat tight around him. The ship rose and fell.

Swee-eesh. Kah-foos. Swee-eesh. Ka-vum. Ka-vum. Ka-vum.

He began to day dream.

He was back in Bermuda. Hitler came to Bermuda. He, James Berkeley, was right in front of Hitler. He was in a position to make a deal.

"You want Jews? Sure, you can have all the Jews. All of them. We've got lots of Jews. They're all English and they are all rich and they all came out here to get away from the war. Some of them own the Bank of England and some of them make soap. You can have them all . . .

"Niggers? Sure, you can have all the niggers. We've got lots. The men work like blacks and the women will let you do *any-thing* to them. The niggers are great, when they wear out their teeth make wonderful necklaces.

"You want the niggers for bayonet practice? Sure, take 'em all.

"Poles? No, we don't have any Poles. Well, maybe I could round-up one or two. Don't worry. I'll find some somewhere.

"Land? Gold? Girls? Sure, you can have it all. Take them. Just don't kill me, that's all.

"My mother? Yes, you can have her, she's old anyway . . . NO. YOU CAN'T HAVE MY SISTER."

No, he couldn't betray his sister or his father. He couldn't. Then his face flushed. At a pinch, he knew, he'd throw his sister into the deal too. Throw them both in.

EVERYBODY BUT ME, he wanted to scream at the waves, the U-boats, the torpedoes, death.

He felt a despair he had never known before . . . There
108

couldn't be anyone in the world as bad as him—he didn't give a blankety, blank, blank, BLANK if everybody on this ship drowned as long as *he* lived.

KLAH-KLAH-KLAH . . .

God, he needed to pee. McIntyre! Now McIntyre again.

ACTION STATIONS. ACTION STATIONS.

He got all the blankets in his lifeboat—even one whose tape came undone. He sat wedged in his perch looking down at the gently heaving after end of the ship. The wake trailed away, a road of even little hills up and down until the uneven surge of the sea broke up the pattern.

He wanted to pee. At Westhill, he remembered, there had been a time when he used to wet his bed every night. Everybody knew he did it but nobody said anything. What they hadn't known and had never found out was that he did it on purpose.

Why? Why had he done it? It wasn't only bad, it was so stupid. How old had he been anyway? It didn't seem all that long ago. And how had he been able to stand it? The mess and everything?

He remembered he would just lie there and let it go. It would be after he had done goo-goos. Every night it was the same. He'd just let it go and feel the warmth of it spread out and around his groin. Sometimes he'd lie in the middle and do it and then afterwards he'd roll over to one side, away from it and go to sleep. Sometimes he'd move way up on one side of his bed, do it, wait for the warmth to pass away and then he'd roll down and sleep in the middle.

He knew other boys wet their beds. He'd heard about it: *they* couldn't help it, he knew that. But he had done it on purpose. Why? It was probably just because he was basically evil—"you're just *basic*ally a L-i-a-r," his sister used to say. There wasn't any other reason he could think of.

And his mother had been so nice; she could have been mad. She had every reason to be mad even though she didn't know he did it on purpose. She was the one who changed the sheets. She never let the maids do it and she never complained, never even mentioned it.

Even now, on the ship, the thought of it left him feeling empty—hollow. Maybe I don't exist at all. Maybe I just imagine I exist.

He had thought for a long time that he was adopted. Finally he told his sister.

"Don't be so stupid—you're the *spitting* image of Daddy."

Well that was all right: he was probably the child of some other woman and their mother had taken him in out of pity.

The sea was so grey, so threatening. He used to paint pictures of ships on bright blue water, water like Bermuda. His mother said he was quite good at painting, "maybe the best of them all," she said. He tried to paint better and better; tried to be the best in the family at painting.

But she didn't seem to pay much attention. In fact, the more paintings he showed her the less interest she seemed to take. He took to painting every spare moment, he turned them out like some madman in the comics turning out bombs.

Since his original compositions didn't seem to interest her so much he took to copying. It was cheating but he'd done it. When that didn't work he took to tracing.

"Yes," she said, "you're pretty good at drawing—run along now."

He took to bigger and bigger sheets of paper and finally he tore pages out of his grandfather's book, *Watercolours of Famous Clipper Ships*, messed them up a bit with his paints and presented them.

She didn't notice the fraud: but his sister did. "Let me have that," she said.

"I did it myself—I *did*."

"Well, let me take it into my room and examine it, James. I'll let you know my decision tomorrow."

She found out. He yelled, screamed his innocence but she

was adamant. He bawled his head off. She wouldn't tell on him, she said, but she wouldn't lie for him either. "But you've *got* to believe me," he wailed. He shouted his innocence so long that he came to believe in it himself. Everyone was against him, it was a dirty plot.

He took to singing. He heard anthems at school—his mother loved music and loved religious music the best—and he hummed them and whistled them all day long to keep them fresh. He rehearsed them all the way home on his bicycle.

At home he'd corner her. "Please, just a minute. I have something for you—something *beautiful*. Listen."

Perched over the after deck James winced. God, how could I have been such a fool—how could I have exposed myself so?

"Yes," she'd say, "I've always loved that anthem—but you didn't get it quite right." Other times she'd stop him. "You're flat—you're singing flat." Sometimes she heard it all the way through without comment. "Did I get it right? Did I?" She'd smile, "Well, almost," she'd say.

"My first three are all musical," he'd hear her say, "James isn't and we can't tell about little George yet."

He remembered why he had gone on and on; it was because when he rehearsed the hymns and anthems to himself they sounded as "true as a bell": he *knew* he had it right—but he didn't.

He looked over the rail and down past Harry's Oerlikon to the sea. It must be forty or fifty feet, he thought. As high as the diving board that Chris, home for the summer holidays, had dived off. His mother was so pleased, "Imagine diving from that height at sixteen," she said.

Teddy jumped. She had liked that too. "But don't try a dive," she said, "jumping is enough at your age."

James went up to the top of the diving board and dove right in. He remembered falling down and down, he remembered thinking, quite cold-bloodedly, that in the next instant he'd probably be dead.

111

She'd been looking the other way. He went and did it again. It sure hurt your head but, what the hell . . . this is a job for Superman.

"Well," she'd said, laughing good naturedly, "as my father is always saying: people say the Berkeleys are brave but there's a great deal of difference betwen being brave and being *foolhardy*—just look at you, James, you look pea-green. Come in and get dry."

Everything good came from the Halcyons and all the bad traits from the Berkeleys. Mother and Christopher and Teddy and little George were like the Halcyons; his sister was in the middle and he was pure Berkeley.

His looks he'd given up on long before. He had a wide turned-up nose: just like that oik Charlie. Charlie looked like a pig, he could see that, and he guessed he did too.

For all he knew he'd end up looking like Hammersmith and McIntyre soon. He remembered she was always saying that George, the baby, reminded her of that Roman who'd seen the British slaves—"not Angles but angels," he'd said. Christopher, as everyone knew, was "distingué"—James agreed with that. Christopher was the best guy on earth. Teddy was the best looking—"an Adonis," she said. Victoria was "a piece of Dresden china."

He used to ask her what he was and she'd say, "You look fine, Jamie. You look your best when you're dressed up." Once, he remembered, she'd even said that the doctor said he had the healthiest body he'd ever seen on a boy.

Well, he might be dumb and ugly but he was healthy and he was a boxing champion twice over—even if it was in the Microbe and then the Mosquito weight—and he *could* do a hundred yards in eighty seconds flat.

But the thought of swimming made him look down at the sea again and that made him shiver—

"God, I've got to pee."

"Harry," he called in a loud whisper. "Hey, Harry." But

Harry couldn't hear him; the wind was blowing the wrong way.

He could pee over the side. But he was bound to be seen. That was impossible. There were only two alternatives, to desert his post and go to the head for which, in wartime, one was shot or to pee in his pants. He decided on the former—but he'd wait another five minutes.

He tried standing up. It helped for a moment and then it was just as bad as before.

He watched the Red Ensign fluttering just up and beyond the figure of the look-out on the mast. They had a flag pole in the stern, why didn't they fly it there?

His father's cabin cruiser flew the Blue Ensign from her stern; a much more handsome flag, he thought.

"Jaysus, there's nothing else for it, I've got to go."

He ran along with his head down. Perhaps if he didn't look at anybody there was a tiny bit more chance that they wouldn't look at him. He got down the first ladder and down the second and then he was running, with little steps because the jarring made him want to go even more, across the after deck, his hand just touching the canvas cover of the cargo hatch.

Then, miraculously, he was inside. He stopped for a moment, and, holding on to the black-out curtain, caught his breath. He could hardly believe his luck.

He started down the companionway. God, he could even go grunts if he was quick.

He tore down his pants, sat on one of the bowls and peed, slowly, luxuriously. He seemed to flow on and on like those little streams that squirted out of the ship's side; like a water tank in a cowboy movie with bullet holes shot in it.

And now, thank you dear God, I can go grunts.

GAR—VOOOOOOOOOOM!

He was knocked clear off the bowl.

So, it's as simple as that, he said to himself, we are torpedoed

113

and he pulled up his pants and when he'd buttoned them he was on deck again.

The world was falling down, there was no doubt about that but why did they have to make so much noise about it?

Brawnk-Brawnk-Brawnk—The Commodore ship's hooter went on and on.

Brawnk-Brawnk-Brawnk—It was insane, it was as if some maniac had got hold of the cord.

And then, just when he got to his post, their ship took it up. BRAWNK-BRAWNK-BRAWNK

The sound semed to pick him up bodily into the air and cast him down again. He stopped his ears and looked about desperately. Harry was waving his arms. The gunner one arm —at Harry. McIntyre was standing for'ard. He seemed to be jumping up and down. No, now he was still. The ship was still moving: indeed now she was veering, perilously again, to port. If anything she was going faster; the whole ship was vibrating now as if she would shake to pieces. The ga-vum of the propeller was faster—like a gallop:

Pavum, p'vum, p'vum, p'vum, p'vum . . .

When the ship started sinking which was the best side to jump? The high side or the low side? Or did you get in a boat? Jump and then get on a raft like McIntyre?

Peh-teck. "This is the—"

BRAWNK

"—Capt'in speaking—"

BRAWNK

"—Billings, belay that fuck—"

BRAWNK

"—noise or I'll crucify you—"

BRa . . .

Peh-teck. "Er . . . hello . . . this is the Capt'in speaking. Remain calm. Ship's company remain at Action Stations. This ship is not hit. I-say-again, this ship is *not* hit. Passengers will

114

kindly remain in the dining saloon. We are proceeding on our normal course—"

He sounds just like the Vicar, James thought.

"—with the utmost despatch." Peh-teck.

We are not hit. Not yet we bleeding aren't. James found himself wedged in his place chewing the paint of the rail.

Harry was sitting down again.

Brawnk-Brawnk-Brawnk. The Commodore ship's hooter grew less raucous. Was it just contrast? No, now it had stopped altogether.

Harry was pointing to starboard. James craned his neck but he couldn't see anything. The Commodore ship is hit, he thought. She's the only one. Yesterday and this morning Harry had said he could smell land . . .

Billings had been blowing the horn. It was Billings' fault . . . the men hated Billings. James didn't think he'd ever seen Billings. Yes, eczema, they said. He remembered the ugly and cratered face of the officer who signed him on; he remembered the dirty-looking flakes on the man's blue jacket. The Captain had cursed him. James wished the Captain had killed him. The men wanted to throw Billings overboard. McIntyre wanted to throw him overboard. He wanted to throw McIntyre overboard.

No, I don't, God—all I want to do is get on dry land. Just one year. Grannie always said the Vicar looked like a pink rabbit—and why do I think of such crazy things . . ?

Pa-vum, p'vum, p'vum, p'vum, p'vum.

You could feel the engine pounding away; you could feel it on your bottom.

Now the wind was blowing right off the stern and behind them their white wake was a perfect curve just as he used to make, on paper at school, with a protracter.

Then he saw the Commodore ship, their sister ship. She was already so far away she looked like a broken toy. Two pieces riding up and down separately. One piece was bigger than the other. The little piece was the bow turned upside down. It looked funny. The bigger piece was the same as them; he could see the very spot, almost, where he was sitting. Their No. 3 boat on the port side was the only one in the water. Ropes trailed down to her. Smoke, dirty black smoke everywhere. Little figures just like ants and little black balls bobbing in the water. Heads. Now you see them, now you don't.

But it seemed a good omen. If their No. 3 boat got away all right maybe the *Empire United*'s would too. Dead ship's name . . .

"Faunty. Are you all right, Faunty?"

"Yes."

Harry was gesturing upwards. James couldn't see anything but the rigging and some sea gulls.

"Shyte-'awks," shouted Harry, "lovely. Shyte-'awks—good sign."

James nodded. "Harry, we're going to stop for them aren't we?" He had to shout it twice against the wind. ". . . aren't we?"

Harry smiled and shook his head.

Just keep shaking, James thought, that's the sweetest shake I've ever seen. But Harry's only a seaman. Say some lousy officer puts us about? But the Captain said . . .

Officers, he decided, were a bunch of shitty blankety-blanks: just like doctors, they never told you anything. But the Captain was all right. He was a good guy—a *good* guy. Besides, to think evil of the Captain was not much different than thinking evil of God—too dangerous.

Just one year, God, after that you can have me. Just one year on land . . .

It was when he had dengue fever that the doctor wouldn't tell. And he'd prayed then too but he couldn't remember the bargain he'd made with God. Probably just to stop the headache; just to let him be well again and he'd never be bad . . . Anything to stop the whirling careening patterns that exploded

116

before him. The patterns that taunted him, pulled him down and into them until he was insane—dying.

His mother said he wasn't dying but then he'd go under again ... And the doctor was there. Dr. Napier, their cousin and very "brilliant" but he wouldn't tell him he wasn't dying.

"Just try to rest. Get some sleep," he'd say. And then he'd see the doctor shaking his head and then they were out of sight but he could hear their voices.

"... keep him quiet ... only case this year ... liquids. Pour liquids into him ..."

"... skinny as a rail, poor lamb ..."

"... the aspirin will help ... lessen the aches too ..."

Yes, the aches. His body ached everywhere as if he were being pulled apart on the rack. Being crushed in his father's rock-crushing machine—run over on the marine railway.

He'd try with all his might to keep from going down, under —but the patterns would get him. They were magnetic.

And he was freezing cold and they kept changing the sheets and piling blankets on him. He'd feel better and then he was freezing again and burning up.

And there were two bad signs. His father being there in the room so often and for such a long time and his mother saying so many things about *him*. Talking about him when he was a baby.

"Born old," she kept saying. "He was born old. Always like a little old man—one side of him anyway ..." And he'd go down again. He couldn't remember what it was like to feel well. Such heaven not to feel sick; why had he never appreciated it? If he had appreciated it, been grateful enough, this would never have happened.

And the other children would come to the door; little George or Vicky and she'd tell them to go away, she didn't have any time for them now, she said. It was one of the best things he'd ever heard.

"We had children who could talk at eleven months—

117

Victoria did. And Christopher could walk at under a year. But this child was walking *and* talking at six months—and whole sentences too. Talking when I was still changing his diapers. I heard birds out under the eaves. To any other child I would have said, 'birdie, hear the birdie?' but not to James —I said, 'James, do you hear the birds?' and he looked me right in the eye and said, 'Yes, they've got nests.' I nearly dropped him. Now how did he know that?"

He didn't care. Just tell me I'm not going to die. But it was good to just be able to call out "Mummy" and she was there instantly. "Don't leave me, *please*," and she said she wouldn't and she didn't.

He'd wake up to find a cold wash-cloth on his forehead. It was good but so soon hot again.

"And that summer," she was saying, "when I took them to Nova Scotia to get out of the heat. He couldn't have been more than eighteen months—no, July, fifteen months. And he was leaning over the side of the ship. George, are you listening?"

"Yes darling, I'm listening."

"And he came and got me, took me over and pointed down to the water. 'Look, Mummy,' he said, 'look down there. It looks as if it's raining, there's even a rainbow. But look, you can look up in the sky and see there are no dark clouds—so it can't be raining. But look down there, it *looks* as if it is.' Those were his exact words and this woman came over—some kind of scientist, you know what I mean. And she said, '*How old* is that boy?' and when I told her she couldn't believe it ..."

And he'd go down into the patterns again and when he came out he'd ask if it was night or day and sometimes it was one and sometimes the other and sometimes he thought he felt worse in the days and sometimes that it was worst at night. But the night was the loneliest and the longest and it was easier, he thought, for death to get you at night.

"Maybe we should have sent him to that special school in Boston," his father said.

118

"George, don't you *dare* smoke in here. Go out if you *must* smoke. No, that school was for *genius* children—he was only an advanced child. Besides, it would have been wasted on him. Look how he turned out when he got to school? Quite ordinary really—couldn't read even until he was almost nine."

"Yes."

"Well, Vicky could read at four and a half."

"I'm going to do something."

"What?"

"I'm going to ask that Marine doctor to come down from Tucker's Island. He'd do it for me, I think. Very bright young man—Dr. Blue."

"No one can be named Blue."

"Well I'll phone. If he can come I'll get him in the boat . . ."

James heard something about a storm and when he came-to there was a stranger there. He had a greeny uniform and blue eyes.

"It's not for nothing they call it Break-bone Fever," he said. His hands were very gentle. James was propped-up. Listened to. Rolled over. Rubbed down. Chilly—funny smell.

"Seven days, eh. You should have called me sooner. Well, we'll see what these can do." Pills rattling in a box.

And James fought back the delirium.

"Sir, will I die?"

"No. You aren't going to die."

"But I feel . . . I'm dying."

"Sonny, that's a part of it. Dengue fever makes you *think* you're dying. Good sign. You're going to get well."

"Sir, I'm afraid."

"Sonny—look at me." The blue eyes, deep and concerned; you could almost *feel* them. "*We* are going to make you well —me and you."

And when he woke up it was morning and the sun was shining in through the curtains and he felt so much better it was like lying on the fluffy cloud again. He could hear birds

119

outside and the sound of the little ferry chuffing up to Salt Kettle. He remembered clearly, he'd seen the doctor sitting there in the wicker chair and he'd said. "Have you been here all night, sir?"

And the doctor said, "Yes sir, I have."

James remembered he'd cried. It must have been the first time he'd ever cried for joy.

Why hadn't he stayed good like that? Why hadn't he stayed grateful? If *only* he had, he wouldn't be here.

"Berkeley," it was Chambers shouting from below.

James looked at his watch: twenty minutes to five and already getting a little dark. He got to his feet. He was very stiff. Maybe Chambers had seen him leave his post? But when he got to the lower deck the Bosun had gone.

Harry gestured towards the galley.

"Get some warm grub in you," Chambers said. "When you're through send McIntyre down. God knows how long we're going to be turned-to this time." He went out carrying a jug and some cups.

Cookie and Newsome were both there working.

"'Ere," said Newsome, "come 'n' get it."

"Thank you."

"Fucking peggies—should be 'ere working. Me, waitin' on peggies."

"Not his fault," said Paddy, who'd just come in. "The Bosun 'as 'em on the boat deck."

"Fuckin' Billings, you mean."

"Yea," said Paddy, "Billings and his blankets."

"I thought it was the Captain." James took the bowl, glad to see it was beans; he could keep beans down, he thought. "McIntyre said—"

"Nah. It's Billings—the fuckin' yellow bastard."

"I'm yellow meself," said Paddy and when he had put his beans down on the table he gave James a pat on the shoulder. "Well, an' how are ya holding out?"

120

"All right. How are you, Paddy?"

"Mustn't grumble, mate. Mustn't grumble—worse things happen at sea, as Harry says." He took a spoon and shovelled in some beans. "Whistle-berries. Now wouldn't you know that black Welshman would be givin' us whistle-berries and us already scared shit-less."

James forced himself to eat. Just like his mother used to say, "it's best to eat and keep your strength up."

More men came in.

"Lovely evenin', in'it?"

"Charming, Mabel. Come 'n' sit by me, love."

"And me standing as a loader for all them bleeding 'ours. Would somebody mind telling me what good a fuckin' Orligun is against a submarine *under* the fucking water—?"

"Turn-it-up."

"—I-ask-you—"

"I did ask Bosun," Cookie said, his eyes wide and bright like Dopey in the Seven Dwarfs, "if I could dump now since Jerry *seems* to know where we are—"

"Pass the sauce."

"—I thought he'd laugh, don'cha' know. But he didn' think it funny at-all."

The tea was as foul tasting as ever. He wished he had some water. No one ever seemed to drink water with meals.

"Christ. That Commodore. 'Orrible, wasn't it?"

"Turn-it-up."

"Well. If we 'ave to end in the boats—"

"BOATS. Them fuckin' things. No oars—I ask you, do the Yanks not know *nuffin'* about the sea—?"

"Don't 'alf give me a turn thinkin' of them bleeding indoor 'andles instead of oars."

"Christ, in a blow, eh? What chance would you 'ave?"

"No oars to steady the boat—'orrible."

"Turn-it-up. Think of the bright side. Without Jerry we'd never 'ave 'eard the Old Man fuck-off Billin's."

121

"Cor. Weren't it lovely? Said 'e'd castrite the bastard—"

"I 'eard the Skipper struck 'im—"

"—I'd like to get 'is balls in a nut-cracker."

James drank some more tea. He needed to go grunts again. If only he'd had time. But it hadn't been very long: didn't he go yesterday? The day before? Well, it wasn't all that long; he'd held it for four days before which proved he could do it again.

"Imagine the Captain talking like that! I could 'ardly believe my ears."

"Billings. Windy bastard. Chroist, what's the sense of them standin' by the boats—we could've 'ad hot char hours ago."

"Eat up and get out—*you* boy, get crackin'!" The man was at the other table. He'd never spoken to James before.

Paddy put his hand over his mouth and whispered. "Better go, lad. Quartermaster."

Outside darkness was closing in on the ship. At first he could hardly see at all and then he was able to make out the horizon and then the white-caps. What lay under them? Sunken ships and drowned sailors . . . The pitiless sea . . . The wind, drying the sweat on his face, felt very cold. The rails were cold to his hands. Where had he left his gloves? The dark sea rolled on. Everywhere he looked, the empty sea. They were alone. Alone.

He found McIntyre by the forward lifeboat, slapping his arms against his body to keep warm. James kept well to the inboard of the deck. There was no one about but them. It could be a ghost ship except for them. The humming vents and the sound of the wind and sea only accentuated the spooki-ness of it all. Maybe McIntyre would be scared now and glad to see him. Why did he hate him so?

"The Bosun said you can go below now—for some char and grub."

"About bleeding time."

"Yes. It's awfully cold, isn't it?"

"You took your sweet time, didn't you."

McIntyre left. James was relieved; he hadn't been friendly but at least he went away. But no sooner had he gone than James wished he'd come back. He felt scared, deserted, homeless. He felt homesick even for his old position by the No. 3 Boat; homesick for the galley. He'd noticed that everytime he moved he was homesick for the place he'd just left. If he could only stay in one place where it was warm and there were people. People and warmth, that was a kind of home.

It was getting darker. No lights anywhere. Just the endless humming and drumming of the ship. Dead ship's name. Dead ship's name.

Why did they have to stay on this deck? What was the point? Surely he could go back to his No. 3 Boat where things were more familiar? Safer? He decided he could. He started down the deck keeping his hand on the rail that ran along the deck-house. To his right the dark void opened up. The sea below: it seemed to be pulling at him again. Pulling him down. Its swishing seemed to be calling to him; laughing at him.

There must be submarines everywhere. There must be. Otherwise why were they still at Action Stations? Maybe, wedged in his perch, he would be able to see some live person. He'd always been afraid of the dark, but this ... Reaching the after rail he could see the R.N. gunner alone at the Oerlikon. James felt better. But the man didn't move: maybe he was dead?

"Hello," he called.

Nothing. The sailor had the cape of his overcoat up. He looked like a monk, a dead monk in some creepy movie. Maybe he'd turn around and have a face turned into a Frankenstein ... maybe even a were-wolf.

He wished he had somebody with him. His father would be best. His father wasn't afraid of *anything*. He was brave. He wished he hadn't sucked-up to his father—but he'd *had* to.

"He certainly knows how to feather his nest, that boy does," his mother often said. It was bad to feather your nest.

But his father really liked him: he was sure of that. It had taken a long time though. His father was strange. Sometimes he wanted to do nothing else but weed the lawn. For hours and hours he'd sit, or kneel, and weed cat's-cradles with a little pronged weeder. All Sunday he'd do it. James worked right along with him, hours and hours. It was crazy but he'd done it. He'd talk. He'd ask his father questions: ask him what he thought he'd like to answer. As soon as his father started saying, "Suppose so" or "I don't know" then James knew he'd asked too much and he'd shut up.

Then it had been photographs. His father got all involved with sorting out photographs. Boxes and boxes of them. Grandfather Berkeley on a gold rush in Canada; Great-grandmother Berkeley in a wicker chair in the Isle of Wight looking as old as a zombie. She'd once been Mary Isherwood, a Lady-in-Waiting, a favourite of the Prince of Wales and very beautiful. But you could never tell about that, Mother said all Berkeleys were liars. Pictures of the First War—millions of them. His father had taken one picture every day. About fourteen different "my best friends" all in uniforms, smiles, their eyes sometimes closed, sometimes popping out. Old planes made out of "pink string and sealing wax", ships, mines, submarines, strange places: Corfu, Alex', Otranto. His father in riding breeches, boots (not looking a bit like Hitler but more like him—James) and a helmet and goggles. Then masses of coloured post-cards with captions underneath: "THE KING AT THE FRONT. At the grave of a fallen hero." "THE KING AT THE FRONT. A chat with peasants." A grey scene, a parson in a white surplice, men in khaki with their backs to you, their feet sticking up like rabbit's ears—kneeling. "Church Services Before Battle." "The poor buggers," his father said sadly. No one knew more about war than his father: his father was just about the only person who had been a soldier, a sailor *and* an airman.

That was why all this junk was very valuable to his father and he'd talk a lot and James worked right along with him until they filled four enormous albums. Every Berkeley since the beginning of time and his father's Life In Pictures.

Weeks and weeks they'd worked. "You're a great help, Sea-Egg—couldn't manage without you." That's what he liked; that's what he wanted to hear.

He worked so hard at so many crazy jobs he got promoted to the nickname Barkus-Is-Willing and he liked that best of all.

On his holidays he followed his father around like a shadow; stuck to him like glue. People said they were as alike as two peas, and he really liked that. His father would go on business trips about the islands in his motor boat. Often he went to the H.M. Dockyard to see "the Captain-in-Charge". James had to wait in the boat, "Unauthorized Persons Not Permitted To Land", for hours on end with nothing more to do than watch a derrick move up and down or count the sea-cockroaches scampering over the dock face. He didn't mind; his father liked him almost as much as he liked Vicky and more than all the others, and that was what he cared about.

He remembered one time when his father had shown that he really *cared* about him.

James had seen some pictures in *Life*. Pictures of starving and homeless Greek children. They had bones showing everywhere and arms and legs like sticks. Some of their stomachs were all withered and some of them all bloated. Their eyes looked out—big, terrified, pleading—from shrunken heads.

Who had done this? Who could do this to children? The Germans, the Germans. There was one picture of a small boy, ragged, deserted, homeless, hungry—an orphan.

James had run with the magazine to his parents. He showed them the pictures. He bawled his eyes out. How could anyone,

125

even the Germans, do this? What had the children done? They were harmless?

He jabbed his finger at the picture of the boy and cried and cried with uncontrollable anguish.

KLING-KLING, KLING-KLING. Six o'clock, his watch said.

It all *proved*, he thought, that there was *some* good in him. He couldn't be all bad because he really had cared about the Greek boy. For weeks afterwards he'd only to remember it to start crying all over again.

"You're a very dear and kind boy to care so much about other people," his father said. He said it over and over: it made James feel warm, good. But the children were real; photographs didn't lie. These children existed and were suffering and dying every day and if it could happen to them . . .

And he wasn't all bad, because, even now when he was in trouble on this stinking ship he still cared about the Greek boy. Didn't he?

But after that he'd slipped back and been really awful. How could one be so good and then be so bad? Because it was after that that he'd gone on the rampage. It was when his father and mother had gone to New York for "a check-up and a rest".

And that's why I'm here and it's what I deserve because . . .

Peh-teck. ALL CLEAR. ALL CLEAR. Peh-teck.

Now he had put the blankets back. It was almost pitch black. Should he try to do it by himself? No, not alone. Wait for McIntyre? Go and find him? Maybe he could leave the blankets until morning and if he was caught-out he'd just say he forgot—he was called on watch. But was he on watch? Past six? Was he on watch at six yesterday? If he was, he wouldn't be today.

For the life of me, he said to himself, I can't remember . . .

He got to his feet. He was so numb he could hardly stand, which was dangerous, he thought, he'd have to watch that. If they were torpedoed . . .

126

"Go help in the galley," a voice said out of the darkness. He was on the lower deck heading for the fo'c'sle. "They're looking for ya."

Who was it? He couldn't see the man's face. "But I'm ... I'm going to the bathroom—head."

"Better piss over the rail, lad, and hop-to at that."

He found a lonely place and peed into the darkness. When they were little they'd pee into the harbour and watch to see if it would make the tide come up. He'd finished before he realized that that wasn't what he wanted.

In the galley Chambers was giving orders. He saw James. His bushy eyebrows frowned. "Berkeley, what are you doing 'ere?"

"Someone said you wanted me."

"You're port—go get some blasted rest."

It was no good, he'd have to own up. "The blankets ..."

"What about 'em?"

"They're still in my boat—I was by myself."

"Blimey—all right," he turned and pointed at some other men. "You two, stow the blankets—port and starboard, GO. Berkeley, get below."

Blimey, thought James, saved by the bell.

When he woke up the next morning the ship was quite still. Even better she was almost silent; no pounding of the screw, only the hum of vents and the distant drone of generators. But he felt very tired. They'd been on watch from midnight to four—the Black Watch, Harry called it—and although all he'd done was sit around the galley, now he felt weak and bloodless, as if he was a convalescent.

"Well, Smith, where do you think we are now? Eh? Navigator, what do ya say?" Jerry Chambers was laughing.

"Luck of this flippin' ship we're back in Bermuda—maybe Bremen for all I care."

"Well, we're snug outside of 'Alifax. In the middle of the biggest bunch of ships you ever did see."

127

"About bleeding well toim," Harry said. "Whoever 'eard of a ship takin' six days from Bermuda to 'Alifax—'Oo can figure that lark?"

"Christ you bastards would sleep through a fuck," shouted one of the R.N. men. "Wakey, wakey, rise and shine; you've 'ad your toim and I've 'ad mine. Come on, show-a-leg there. Eggs and bacey for breakfus'—"

"Fuck-off."

James was surprised to discover that he felt hungry. I may even be able to go to the bathroom, he thought. Everyone will go up to see Halifax and if I pretend to be asleep I can sneak to the head . . .

What watch did they have today anyway? The system was too confusing. The only really safe way to tell was to watch Harry and Paddy; when they turned-to, he did.

"Wakey, wakey goldy-locks, drop your cocks and grab your socks."

There were all kinds of watches. First dog and second dog; port and starboard—why should there be a left-hand and a right-hand watch? It was safer to watch Harry. Hard enough to tell port from starboard and he did that by keeping the aspirin bottle full of brandy—"Nothing will happen but you better have this just in case," his father had said—in the left hand pocket of his overcoat. Brandy is a drink and so is Port. "If you are ever in a life-boat and feel faint, take a sip," his father had said. "But don't touch it unless you really have to."

"Captain's inspection at noon and I want this place spotless. I want everything spotless."

"Fuck the Captain." Harry, in a falsetto voice.

"Who said that?"

"After you with the Captain, love," piped Paddy.

"Was that you, Smith?" Chambers went towards Harry's bunk.

"You? Who?" Paddy squeaked from above.

Chambers looked up.

"Yoo-hoo," echoed Harry from below.

"I'm warning you lot. Any more and I'll 'ave you."

"Ya carn't," piped someone down the line, "I've gotta left 'and pipe."

"It's no matter to me—we'll try another way—as long as you 'aven't got trench mouth, Mabel darling."

"That bleeding Mabel—nothing but excuses, told me 'er 'ands was chapped."

"I'll have no more of this," said Chambers. "Levity—that's all I ever get from you lot, *levity*." He went up the companion-way and, from his bunk, James could see he was laughing.

Halifax, he thought. We're here. There may be a whole Atlantic ahead but we're here. And a big convoy was safe, Chambers had said so. Stands-t'-reason, lad, don't it?

V

The land, Halifax, lay over to the starboard. There were patches of snow on the slopes of the hills making everything look black and desolate. It was all too far away to seem anything like home—real soil—and they weren't going ashore anyway. But that it was there at all proved that land existed: a fact that James had come to question.

There were ships everywhere. Some big, some small, some new with thick smokestacks like theirs and a lot old with tall thin stacks like exaggerated versions of Mr. Lincoln's hat. They were all grey but some of them so dark they looked black just as the *Empire United* had done when he first saw her.

Off their port beam was a great pale-grey three-stacked liner. At first James thought she might be the *Monarch* or the *Queen of Bermuda* but Harry said "no, P 'n' O", and James thought she might be *The Reina del Pacifico* that Chris and Teddy used to travel on to school before the war. She had a swimming pool and an electric horse that could walk, trot, canter and gallop and a punching-bag on a spring.

Maybe she wasn't *The Reina* but he'd pretend she was. He wished he was on her: in a cabin by himself with his own bathroom. Or, best of all, sharing a cabin with Christopher. Christopher took care of you and he never lost his temper like Teddy. But a bathroom . . .

His trip to the head had been something of a disaster. He'd

130

no sooner sat down when an R.N. sailor came in, looked around, winked, took down his bell-bottoms and sat on the end bowl. James tried to look straight ahead; he felt himself blushing and he couldn't stop.

It really wasn't right that you couldn't go to the bathroom by yourself. He supposed "they" had done it just to be mean; if they wanted to just keep an eye on things they could have built partitions off the floor the way they were at school— and that was disgusting enough, everyone smelling everyone's stink.

The sailor gave himself a quick—and to James's mind, a totally inadequate—wipe, pulled up his trousers, lit a cigarette and sauntered out. There wasn't even a place to wash your hands, you had to go next door and nobody seemed to . . . then two smells hit him at once, the man's dirt and the cigarette. He had to get up and out before he was sick.

He'd figured out, long before it seemed, that the time to go was after a watch-change in the night. To come off watch and wait until his watch-mates had fallen asleep. He'd tried but he always fell asleep himself: well, he damn well wouldn't to-night.

Now, over to the starboard, the sun shone steely-white out of the grey overcast. It seemed little brighter than a flashlight; a flashlight in the daytime.

"That bastard," said Harry pointing to a little black ship with its funnel in the stern like a tanker. "She can't make four knots with a wind up 'er arse. Bloomin' coaster—a tramp. Chroist, what'll they dig up next—Thames barges?"

"Jaysus," said Paddy.

"Look at them little things."

"R.C.N. motor launches," said Harry's gunner. "Not much use."

"Christ, there must be a hundred ships, eh?"

"More like fifty."

"Let's count then."

131

"Look. Can't be—is that *Charribus*?" Harry.

"Nah. Same class maybe but not 'er," said the gunner. "Those old destroyers can't steam far, you know. A thousand miles at most—and the bloomin' route we've come she'd 'ave 'ad to put back long ago."

"I said we went over by the Azorees, didn't I Paddy china?"

"You can say that again."

"Look, there's a new destroyer, in'it?"

"Corvette."

"Pretty, isn't she."

"I tell you that's *Charribus*. I'd recognize—"

"Look at that lovely cruiser."

"Corvette, you hidiot."

"Smashin', in'it?"

James had counted forty-three but he wasn't sure.

"Signals there, look."

"What'd 'e say?"

"Sixty-seven, 'e said."

"Must be code."

"Look up there—we're answering."

"What's 'e say?"

"Jerry won't mess with this lot, eh?"

"Sixty-seven—"

"Fuck, they won't," said the gunner. "They'll tackle any-think: wolf-packs they call 'em. Four or six—sometimes a dozen subs 'it you at once from all sides—"

"Turn-it-up . . . I just 'ad me breakfast."

"—proper confusion, I-can-tell-ya. That German admiral, 'e's a smart basket. What's 'is name? Doan-blitz?"

"Doughnuts," said Harry.

"Doenitz, I believe," said James.

"Dough-balls, Go-balls and No-balls—"

"Cor, that's it. 'Ow'd you know, sprog?"

"Because my father told me—he captured him in the first war."

132

"Is that right?"

"There 'e goes again—bleeding little liar."

"No foolin'?"

"He did. It was in the Strait of Otranto—"

"*Christ 'e can lie.*"

"It's the truth. He even has a pistol Doenitz gave him—a Mauser."

"*Liar.*"

"I'm not. It was the *biggest* submarine in the German navy."

"Is that right?"

"Submarines weren't even invented back that far."

"They certainly were—they had a submarine in the American Civil War—"

"Man the pumps, mates—the shit's gettin' too thin for the shovel."

"Pity your father didn't kill the bastard, eh Faunty?"

"Yes," said James, "the dirty bugger."

The Captain came down the companionway backwards like everybody else—which surprised James—except that he moved faster, as if his feet were wheels. He came down like little George sliding down the bannister.

Billings, the first officer, followed. Billings's mottled face was a pale grey, quite "colourless" his mother would have said.

The Captain inspected the R.N. men first. Standing at attention in their blue uniforms they made the rest of the ship's company look like ragamuffins.

"Fine body of men, Chief," said the Captain. "Very grateful to have you with us. Carry-on." He moved on to Chambers. "Sorry about the crowding—can't be helped, I'm afraid." The Captain's head only came up to Jerry's shoulder. "What's this? Have that attended to, Mr. Billings." He was getting closer.

James blushed. The Captain was looking him up and down.

133

His eyes were bloodshot and watery-looking but they were eyes that seemed to know something you didn't: that probably knew something about yourself that you didn't. He turned and looked at Billings quizzically and then back at James. "Who're you?" he said in a quiet pained voice.

"Berkeley, sir."

"This is the lad working his way over, sir," said Billings.

The Captain looked James over again from his shoes up to his sports jacket (his overcoat was folded and laid out on his bunk with his life-jacket) his shirt and tie and then into his eyes again. "Over to school?" he said, "what school?"

"The Elms, sir."

"—?"

"It's at Littlehampton, sir."

"Doesn't matter where it is." He turned and looked at Billings again.

Now Billings looked at James. His eyes were nervous and peculiar-looking; then James realized that they were such a dark brown that you couldn't see a dividing line between the iris and the pupil. He'd never seen eyes like them before.

"I thought he was going to be an apprentice, sir. At some dockyard or something."

James bit his lip to keep from laughing: Harry had said Billings had eyes "loik two piss-'oles in the snow". He couldn't remember snow very well but he'd seen piss-holes in Bermuda's sand often enough and that was just what Billings's eyes looked like.

"Enough," the Captain had already said. "Well, then, Berkeley, how do you like the *Empire United*?"

"Very well, sir," he kept rigidly at attention and tried to answer the way Christopher would.

"Bosun taking care of you?"

"Oh, *yes*, sir."

The Captain's face was very wrinkled and his ears stuck out like soup-ladles—"Ears" Jones.

134

"Be so kind as to write down one word, Mr. Billings—Berkeley." He moved on.

James let his breath out. The Captain came back. James drew his breath in again.

"When did you last change that shirt?"

"—"

"Well?"

"I haven't, sir—not since I left home."

The Captain's face creased even more. "Chambers, see this lad gets a clean shirt." He moved on again. "Well, McIntyre, enough action for you?"

"Yes sir."

"Something to tell your grandchildren about. Eh?" He pushed open the door of the showers, peered in and then let the door close.

"What's your name?"

"Lafferty, sir."

"Orangeman?"

"County Cork," said Paddy loudly. "Begging your pardon, sir."

"Well, be sure and tell them when you get back how much Queenstown cost us."

"Cobh, sir."

"Quite so." The Captain moved on. "Smith, isn't it?"

"Yessir."

"Miss your beer, Smith?"

"Not 'alf—but we all do, sir."

"Quite," said the Captain. He walked on, and, mounting the companionway, he went up as he came down—as if on wheels. Billings bounced after him.

"Phew."

"Cor—Paddy, you ain't 'alf got a nerve."

"Ribbing the Old Man. Coo! What'd it mean anyway?"

"'Miss-your-beer, Smith'." Harry. "Christ, 'e can talk."

135

"Yeh, did you see 'im come on board at Baltimore—talk about *pissed*."

"Bermuda too—first ashore, last on board—pissed as a fart."

"Ah, t'is a good man's weakness," said Paddy. "I wouldn't hold it against him—"

"Nar, you'd put it up him, you Irish sod—"

"Faunty—you filthy little Peggy you—nearly got us all in dutch."

He only had two shirts in his suitcase and he was saving one for London. His mother said to put on a clean one for London.

"What did 'e write your name down for?" Hammersmith asked.

"I don't know."

"Hell 'e don't. The Capt'in's gonna fix 'im up with a soft job," said McIntyre, "you see if 'e don't. Snots are all the same. Well, good riddance is what I say."

"Leave 'im be—"

"McIntyre, shut up." The Bosun pushed by them. "Berkeley, change your shirt."

"But be sure and put your tie back on," said Hammersmith. "The Captain might ask you up for afternoon tay."

In the afternoon James had just settled in his place by the life-raft when he heard his name being called.

It was the young officer he'd seen walking on the deck. "Are you Berkeley?"

"Yes."

"Well, come with me. The Captain wants you."

James followed him. It was frightening: like going to see the Headmaster at school. They went forward, up ladders, down passages and through water-tight doors. Then they were in a part of the ship where the floors were all covered with brown linoleum. It seemed very luxurious after steel. The air smelled of wax and everything seemed very clean.

136

They stopped outside a door which was propped open. There was a pale brown curtain across the opening and a small cocoanut door mat on the floor—just like a house.

The officer knocked.

"Come."

The officer gestured for James to go in and then turned and walked away.

The Captain was sitting at his desk writing something. His cap was off, he was bald. It was a very cosy cabin: books, a bed-spread, a carpeted floor—even pictures.

"What is it?" The Captain didn't look up.

"Berkeley, sir."

"Just a moment, Berkeley."

James looked about again: A photograph of a sailing ship; a carafe of water with a glass upsidedown; a photograph in a little silver frame—a woman and two children and a dog. James decided that the Captain was a gentleman: or "almost a gentleman", as his mother would have said. He wondered, though, how he had saved all these things when his last ship went down.

The Captain raised his head. "Well, Berkeley, sit down. Sit down there."

It was an arm-chair. James sat down on the edge of it.

The Captain just looked at him. After what seemed a long time James gestured towards the little picture. "We have a dog just like that, sir, a springer—at home, we do."

"Yes. Oh, yes."

Well, that hadn't worked.

"Berkeley..." he drummed his fingers on the desk: A signet ring just like Dad's, a gentleman definitely. "What school did you say you were going to?"

"The Elms, sir—but I go to Fotheringham after that—where my brothers went."

That worked.

"Yers. Quite, quite. Your father builds boats, doesn't he?"

137

"Yessir. Fairmiles now, sir."

"I understand—but don't give away military secrets, eh?" He smiled and took out a cigarette tin. English cigarettes, Harry would like those; no, the cigarette said Lucky Strike. But it was an English tin, worn and battered. 555 it said. "Doesn't your father think it's a bit risky—to travel, I mean?"

"Well . . . my father said if you miss your public school education you miss everything—sir."

"I suppose so." He drummed his fingers again. "How old are you, boy?"

"—"

"I know what it says here—but how old are you really?"

"Thirteen." Safest bet.

Silence.

Even the way the man smoked was a pleasure after the fo'c'sle . . . James felt that he could watch him forever.

"Tell me, are you managing all right down below?"

James hesitated. He had the feeling that if he said no, the Captain would do something about it. But the man seemed to want him to say yes. Besides, as Chris said, "never give in, never"; and Dad said "a gentleman never shows fear . . ." "Sort of, sir."

"Chambers watch out for you?"

"Yes sir."

"Good man, Chambers."

The chance had gone.

"They keep you busy?"

"Yes sir."

"That's good. Always best to have something to do. What is it you do?"

"Well . . . in the galley, sir . . ."

"A peggy, eh?" He laughed again. "Well, it'll be something to tell your grandchildren about. Eh?" His face had a pained look; James knew he wished he hadn't said it.

138

"I think it would be a good thing, Berkeley, if you had a good wash'n'brush-up. Get yourself a shower."

"Yes sir."

"Well, if there's anything I can do for you, Berkeley, just let me know—" There was a knock on the door. "Come."

An officer with his cap under his arm. "Signal, sir, from the Commodore."

"Thank you." He opened it, read it and put it down on the desk. "That's all, Benson." He turned back to James. "Well now, is there anything . . . anything at all?"

"Yes, sir. I'd like a towel and a wash-cloth—"

"A what? Good Lord, Berkeley—why didn't you ask Chambers?"

"—"

"Well?"

"I didn't like to, sir."

"Yes, I see." He reached up and pushed a button.

They waited.

"What have you been using—for a towel?"

"My handkerchief, sir."

"Sir," a head popped around the curtain.

"Steward. Bring a towel and a face flannel, will ya."

"Right away, sir."

"Well . . . all I can say is . . . if the going gets a bit rough for you—down below, I mean, you can come up here and find me."

James smiled and nodded.

"You understand?—oh, thank you, steward."

James took the towel and wash-cloth. "Thank you, sir." He got up.

"You'll be able to find your way? I mean—back here if you want me?"

"Yes sir."

"Or else the bridge."

"Yes sir. Thank you very much, sir."

"Well then, run along."

James had the wash-cloth in his pocket and the towel stuffed under his coat.

"What did 'is nibs want?" asked Hammersmith.

"Nothing."

"Get-out-of-it—what?"

"Just asked for my father's name and address."

"Don't believe ya. What you got there anyway?"

"Just my towel," James said nonchalantly.

"Let's see.

He pulled it out and started for his locker.

"No—what did 'e want?"

"Oh, pipe down 'Ammersmith—none of your business."

"Come on, tell us."

"'E 'ad 'im up for a little port 'ole drill, that's what—so pipe down. Go on, 'Arry, tell us about the tanker. Was it really capsized—right over like?"

"There wasn't nothing stickin' out except this stern-section see—over almost complete. Like this."

"Coo, lummee. And you was stuck inside?"

"Yeah, four of us see. In the bleedin' galley—a break 'n' all, since we 'ad bags of grub and water. But talk about scared—Christ-all-bleeding-moighty. See, when she was 'it she must of twisted 'erself. All the doors was jammed. Couldn't budge 'em—not a chance and us trapped in there upsidedown 'n' all. And just the arse of the ship out of water—see, well, it could slip under any moment we thought—"

"No port 'oles?"

"Coming to that. One, see, one regular port-hole. First I didn't want to open it at all—you know, I thought if the air got out, well, down we go to Davey Jones. But we 'ad to try and get out and my old china, Wells—'Oley Wells we called 'im —poor blighter dead and gone now. Appendicitis took 'im—"

"'Pendicitis—a 'orrible way to go."

140

"Yeh, I never stop thinking about it—everytime I leave 'ome."

"Cor, when do you think they'll put doctors on ships? It ain't *right*."

"Never, mate. Not for the likes of us."

"Pipe down. Go on 'Arry."

"Well, 'Oley says—Christ he was a funny basket—'Oley says, 'For what came we out for to sea—to die?'—'e was always saying that over'n'over—'Come on,' 'e says, 'one of us matelots 'ave got to get through.'"

"Well all you'd do is fall in the water, wouldn't ya?"

"I'm coming to that. First off we got two dish towels outside, looped over the rail—distress signal. See, our biggest fear was from our own blokes. Middle of a shipping lane, floating wreckage—Christ, the Royal Navy might shell us and sink us anytime—not to mention the Jerries. So we 'ad to get this signal up to let 'em know we was trapped there. But the towels kept blowing away. So someone 'ad to get out there.

"Anyway, 'ave you 'eard that malarky about a man can get through any 'ole he can get 'is 'ead through—balls. I tried. Christ how I tried. Took all me clothes off—no good—rubbed meself down with butter. Fuck-all—couldn't even get me shoulders through."

"But if you got out what would you stand on?—upsidedown and all?"

"Plan was, see, to rig a sling hanging from the pipes of the deck above us and the rail—outside. Well, I couldn't get through and I was the smallest—save for the boy, see.

"Oh, I forgot to mention this 'orrible bangin'. It must 'ave been all the doors under water—or part under. The ship would bounce up and down and everytime she went up all these doors banged. Bang. Bang. Bang. Eerie. Frightening—like there was men down there slammin' 'em. And then the ship would go down and all the doors would bang again. Then too, there was this 'orrible 'issing—wheezing. It was the air, you

141

know, being sucked in and out. Chroist it pretty near drove us crackers—"

"God's-stroooth, 'ow long were you in there?"

"Nineteen days—"

"*Nineteen days!*"

"Not a word of a lie—nineteen days. Well, I tell you, we took this boy see—the nipper. Poor little lad, skinny though he was he wouldn't fit through. Stripped 'im down bare-arsed naked and tried to shove 'im through. Not a sausage—three of us shovin' and 'im squealing his 'ead off—but 'e wouldn't fit through.

"But we gotta get somebody out—to tie up a signal and to wave like. 'Starve the little basket,' says I.

"'And don't give 'im no water,' says 'Oley, 'hit's liquids that make you fat—I read about it in the paper.'

"So we starved the poor little bloke. Starved 'im for days.

"Forgot to say—on the second day, to add to our troubles we began to 'ear another, a different banging—right under our feet on the ceiling. Rap, rap, rap. Someone in there and no mistake. Tap, tap, tap, goes I. Rap, rap, rap, 'e says. 'Fuck,' say I, ''ow can we get 'im out?' and then I saw this axe.

"'For what came we out for to sea?' says 'Oley Wells, 'to die?—you open up a 'ole in that and then the air escapes and then we've 'ad it for sure.'

"Well, we argued back and forth and finally Wells—my china—takes this axe and says 'e'll make a start at a 'ole. Well, 'e busts the axe with the first blow—did it on purpose, I expect —although I don't like to speak evil of the departed. But at the time, I-don't-mind-telling-ya, I was bleeding grateful."

"But, 'Arry, what 'appened to the poor bloke stuck in there?"

"Still there, mate."

"Coo. Did 'e go on tappin'?"

"Did 'e! He tapped and tapped and banged and banged. He'd stop awhile and then 'e'd start again. Drove us damn

near crazy. Then 'e started tappin' in code. Christ it was
'orrible! 'Save my soul', he kept tappin'. Then on the seventh
day he stopped and we 'eard no more out of 'im."

"Coo. That's 'orrible, in'it?"

"See, he didn't 'ave any water or food like we did, poor
bloke. We figured 'e was in the 'ead—but 'e wouldn't 'ave got
much water being upsidedown and all."

"Well, 'ow did you get water then?"

"First thing I did was drain the water out of the pipes into
pots—there was a lot of it, too. Never did use it all."

"Christ, 'ow did you shit?"

"Garbage can—got proper ripe too—I can tell ya. No lid,
'n' all.

"Well this 'issing and banging of doors went on and on and
we kept starving the poor boy. Finally, after about ten days,
I think it was, we stripped 'im bollocks naked, rubbed 'im all
over with butter again and shoved. 'E popped right through.

"Then we got 'im to rig this sling and he sat there as pretty
as you please. 'E asked for a drink first and my china says,
'You 'ave a drink and you won't fit back tonight.' 'Shit,' the
boy says, 'I'm never coming back in there with you lot.' Well,
then 'e asked for his clothes—he was shivering the poor little
perisher."

"Where were you anyway?"

"I told you—Bay of Biscay. But winter time, mind. Forty
it was—after Dunkirk—November. 'E just wouldn't come
back in—out there for over a week but 'e'd never even try to
come back.

"Cold! Cold as the tip of an Eskimo's tool. Christ knows
'ow 'e felt out there—we was perishin' inside. And nights,
mates, no fuckin' lights and all that ghostly bangin'. Near
drove us balmy.

"Then we saw a ship. Christ we yelled—but it weren't any
good of course. But they saw the nipper waving and they sent
over a boat."

"'Ow'd they get you out?"

"Well, they took the nipper first and went back. They went out of sight too—Christ we thought they were going to leave us. One of our blokes was for 'anging 'isself if they didn't come back. We were proper done-in, I-can-tell-ya. But they came back and cut us out in no time."

"Why didn't you cut yourselves out with the axe?"

"Don't be daffy—that little thing—besides it was busted. We'd tried that—don't you worry. But they 'ad a real cutter—oxy-'cet, the works. Cut a 'ole in the door. But nineteen days, mates . . ."

"Well, if I'd been through that lark you'd 'ave never got *me* back to sea again."

"Yeah, 'Arry, why'd you ever come back?"

"Funny thing about one bloke—a Liverpool lad 'e was—'e didn't want to leave. It was 'is turn to go through the 'ole and 'e wouldn't go. 'I want to stay with Auntie,' 'e kept saying. 'E'd got so used to the place 'e didn't want to go, I'spose. Finally 'Oley slapped 'im. 'Auntie,' he kept saying but 'e went down."

"Fuckin' arse'oles, 'Arry. Why'd you ever come back to sea again?"

"That's the question, lad, in'it? Why? Funny, we all did. Every last one of us. It's like old 'Oley Wells used to say, 'For what came we out for to sea?' Cor, 'e was a one was my old china."

Tonight he wouldn't make a mistake. As soon as they were asleep he'd get to the head. Afterwards he'd go and have a shower; but what about the money pouch? Someone might see it. Maybe he could hang it over the taps; but it might get wet. Best to hide it in his clothes and keep his eye on them. But it would be good to go to the bathroom. The whole North Atlantic was ahead and he didn't know when he'd get another chance.

"Eh, Faunty. 'Ow about giving us a banana?"

"No. Sorry, Harry, I can't. They aren't mine."

"Cor, they look to be getting ripe 'n'all, now."

"Yeh. You'll never get 'em to Blighty."

"But my father sent them as a present."

"You liar," said McIntyre, "'Oo to, then?"

"To his agent—Mr. John Somers."

"Coo—to his flippin' agent, 'e says. Mr. flippin' Somers—"

"Leave 'im be," said Paddy.

"Yeh. It's 'is bananas, after all." Harry.

"And the mean little snot would sooner let 'em go bad than share 'em with us."

"No. I promised—"

"Fuck you then."

"No. If—"

"You 'eard."

"Leave 'im."

"They're all the same them fucking snots."

"Captain's darling."

"I can't help it," he'd heard his mother say as he hid behind the sofa. "I can't help it and I *must* say it—sometimes I think he's possessed by devils."

"Don't be ridiculous."

"Well, it happens, you know. You only have to read the New Testament—"

"Oh, come now. Just an overdone case of boys will be boys."

"I've no other explanation, he's possessed by devils. If only there was a decent Anglo-Catholic priest—"

His father groaned but he himself thought his mother might be right. But it wasn't devils, it was *himself*. He, James, really got a kick out of going berserk. It was bad and you felt *scared as hell* when you did it and guilty afterwards: but it was fun, there was nothing more exciting.

He and Charlie and Bully Fitch and a crowd of others:

145

especially the Craig boys, who were older and knew all sorts of tricks.

After pretending to go to bed, he'd get dressed and sneak out. He'd climb across the upstairs veranda, over the roof of the maids' quarters and away.

They terrorized the whole Parish. The Craig boys invented The Electric Door Knocker. Black thread tied to a door knocker and they hid in the shrubbery and pulled the thread. Knock-knock-knock. A man or a woman would come to the door. Peer out, scratch their heads and then go back. Wait a few minutes and do it again—sweating with anticipation in the bushes. Two or three times and the men (the women usually locked the door after the first time), with newspapers or pipes in their hands, would get mad and start yelling, cursing into the darkness . . .

Bully Fitch had a refinement. First time a grown-up caught on they threw a Jew-cracker in the door.

They had the mixture perfect now and wrapped in stout brown paper taped with sticking plaster. Samson Sausage and you had to be careful with the gun-powder dunked toilet paper wick.

Ga-voom.

And by the time the people knew what had happened they had "peezed through the trees".

"Peeze for the trees, men!" and then they'd scatter and meet later in their hide-out and smoke and talk about it. Afterwards they chewed fennel, to kill the smell, and sneaked home.

James himself invented The Welding Job. Short length of pipe, blocked at one end, filled with gunpowder and held with a wire handle. Lit, it operated like a blow-torch and was excellent for obliterating the names of houses on varnished or painted signs.

Ftzzzzzowmmm! and nothing left but smoking charcoal.

The Spook Fire Dance was Charlie's idea. It was meant to

146

frighten coloured people but they used it on anyone who came along. A thick trail of gunpowder across the road. They hid behind the wall, matches ready, waiting. Someone coming.

"Cannibal or Cavalier?"

"Cannibal."

Ftzowzow-zow-foom. Right in front of the bicycle—and the cannibal "took-off" often yelling to "beat the band".

They carried slingshots from which they shot steel staples: James stole them from the ship yard. They could bust a street lamp at thirty paces; shooting together, Gatling gun, they could shatter a twelve-paned window in one volley. Brat-tat-tat-tat-tat. That sweet moment of destruction; the sheer joy of it. And then the short-lived, but deep, peace of accomplishment afterwards.

It was War; war on all adults and it was delicious.

The Craig boys even wanted to raid their *own* house. They were tough. They had a step-father with one leg who beat them with his crutches.

"But your *mother*."

"O.K., to hell with it. How about that Stubbs's house?"

"You mean that nutty American millionaire?"

"Yeah. They're away—we could break in."

"His name is Carbon Gasolene Stubbs."

"You're lying?"

"I'm not. His father christened him that because that's how he made his money. My old man told me."

"Your old man's a liar." Craig boy.

Dukes up. "You take-that-back." Chris's code: fight anyone who insults the family—especially Mother or Dad. Fight 'em however big; and *never* give in.

"Take-it-back yourself."

"Take-it-back and right now!" Chris once fought two coloured boys by himself. He took an awful licking but he never gave in.

"O.K., Mickey. I take it back. I was only fooling."

147

"Come on, you guys."

They broke into the Stubbs's house and the six of them drank two cases of warm coke. They smoked and threw the bottles in the fireplace, the bathtub, all over the joint . . . The Craig boys started smashing them down the brick steps into the garden and then lobbing them—hand-grenades—into the empty swimming pool. Kah-pow! Smash! Then they heard the caretaker and they peezed through the trees.

Saturday night was their "night to howl". It went on for months and months.

The night they frightened the horse with the Fire Dance James had quit.

"You sissy."

He didn't care what they said; they were good and scared too and he knew it.

That was the night that Sergeant Gantry came to their house. James heard him knock on the door. He'd only just got home himself. He jumped into his pyjamas and ran to little George's room. He looked down over the front steps.

His father and the sergeant talked for some time. James couldn't hear much until his father raised his voice.

"Well, it couldn't have been our children—they've all been in bed for hours."

"Look, sir. I'm sorry—we had a good description and it sounded like your boy."

"Well, you're mistaken. *Goodnight*, sergeant."

It was very loyal of his father to cover for him, he thought, shivering. But he'll be up in a minute: he knows I said I was going to the movies.

Sure enough he saw his father go down the steps towards the bicycle shed. He's checking. He'll find my bike and then he'll come up . . . better to get it from Dad than from the cops.

But his father never came up. And the next day he'd heard them talking.

"I can't do *a thing* with him. Can you imagine any of our other children doing these things? I tell you, he's possessed."

"Oh stop." His father sounded tired, exasperated.

"Well, what can we do?"

"He should be in boarding school . . ."

"If we don't get him out of here soon he won't be accepted at Fotheringham. He'll never pass the exams."

"Terrible to miss out on a public school education."

KLING-KLING-KLING.

What time was it. 9:30 said the luminous dial. Twelve whole pounds his father paid for his watch. He must love him to spend all that money.

But that Sunday had been when the talk of boarding school began. Then he remembered . . . his stomach seemed to fall away, downwards, that same feeling . . . *He* had done it. He himself had begged and begged them to send him to school in England. Why? Why? There wasn't any explanation. It was all too impossible.

Do something. Do anything. Even the Captain said to keep busy. The fo'c'sle was quiet now.

Snoring over the sound of the generators. He climbed down stealthily. He got his towel and wash-cloth and went to the head.

Stifling hot, but empty. Grey walls, no portholes, smells. He knew the ship was still but she felt as if she was rolling.

Oh, God, to be trapped in here. Ship upsidedown. Tap, tap on the floor which would be the ceiling. No one would hear. The water from the bowls would fall on your head.

No one's going to rub *me* down with butter.

He sat down and again wondered at the smallness of his knees, the silly babyish hair on them. It worked, he sighed with relief.

Afterwards he went next door for a shower. He'd forgotten clean underwear. If he went back to his locker he might wake someone up . . . to hell with it.

149

You've got to stop swearing.

He climbed out of his clothes and quickly pulled the tapes and chamois pouch over his head and then stuffed them in a shoe.

The shower was strange, not two taps but one lever. He looked back checking his things and then turned the lever to "warm".

At home they didn't often take showers—although his father always did—just baths. In the summer when the water tanks were low they were only allowed three inches. You always had to be careful of water and not flush the lavatory too often. Sometimes he saw blood in the bowl in his mother's bathroom. It terrified him. She must be dying. He watched her very carefully and then he forgot it. Then he'd see it again. He didn't know what it was and you couldn't ask about things like that.

Back in his bunk his watch said 10:10. He had his overcoat on again under the blanket. They'd be on watch at midnight.

He tried to sleep but everytime he closed his eyes he seemed to see the patterns again: the ones he saw when he had Dengue Fever. It was funny, he thought, the way, now, anytime he felt sick—or even got a headache—he saw the same patterns. He recognized them and they were always the same, taunting him, teasing him, pulling him down like a magnet, and they were nothing like any shapes of the real world. Where did they come from?

And the ship would be sailing soon. They'd be leaving Halifax. It might happen any moment. And then the alarm bell again and the blankets and the water below . . . think of something, *anything*.

He ought to say his prayers. "God bless Mummy and God bless Daddy and Christopher and Teddy and Vicky and little George." He God-blessed all twelve dogs on the estate, the four cats, the horses, the pony and Daisy and the other cows;

Yvonne the house-broken pig, little George's kid goat and all the servants. Then he went right through the crew including McIntyre and Billings. The whole Merchant Navy, the Royal Navy, the Royal Canadian Navy—even the U.S. Navy.

Then he thought he'd better bless all the people he'd been horrible to, especially those he didn't like. Just to be safe. One couldn't take any chances.

Yes, even the Fieldings; those crumby, rotten, lying Fieldings.

That had really been "the straw that broke the camel's back", as his mother said. The Fieldings came to live at their house. Mother and Dad had gone to New York on the flying boat for "a rest and a check-up".

Why had he behaved so badly? What was the excuse? Just because Bill Fielding bossed them around and acted like the "Lord of the Manor" when all he really was was one of the crumby staff in Dad's office?

Yes, that was part of it.

But that strange and awful hollowness as soon as his parents had gone: a feeling as if your bones were rotting away.

"I can't *stand* that woman," Vicky said. "Did you hear the way she talked to poor old Matilda?"

"And he sits in Dad's chair—"

"His head makes a mark on the back—he uses HAIR OIL. And last night he put his *feet* on Mummy's little table."

"He drinks Dad's whisky."

"And all those dreadful programmes they listen to on *our* radio. I know just what Grampy means now: I like the top drawer and I can take the lower drawer but God save me from the middle classes."

The second day, before the Fieldings got home, James got open the back of the big Pye radio and snipped the two wires to the loudspeaker.

A few hours later Bill Fielding called him down from his room. To his surprise the radio was playing.

"Someone cut the wires and I think we both know who it was?"

James fixed him with an icy stare. "I don't know what you're talking about—and kindly stop using my mother's Lowestoft bowl for an *ash*-tray." He turned on his heel and left.

An armed truce followed but a week later the Fieldings threw a party. They rolled up the carpet in the drawing-room and danced. Disgusting.

Vicky locked herself in her room.

James went down to the bicycle shed and did a Wiring Job on every strange bicycle there. It was simple: you just took a pair of pliers, snipped a few spokes and wrapped them around the forks. That bike would never roll again—not on that wheel —next, please.

He really shouldn't have done it. Why? Why?

Fielding said he'd call the police if anything else happened. He said he'd make a deal: if nothing else happened he wouldn't mention *anything* when James's mother and father got home. Otherwise . . . They shook on it.

He and Vicky and George went to Hamilton to meet the Imperial Airways tender. They were very excited; they skipped along, laughing and joking. They waited all afternoon. Nothing came. They waited until it was almost dark. Then they went home, desolate.

James wanted to go back to Hamilton, after supper, on his bike. Bill Fielding said, no.

James went. He had to see his mother and father; not only to be *with* them when they first encountered the Fieldings; he *had* to see them the moment they got to Bermuda. He couldn't wait a second longer; he couldn't be apart from them any more. He waited and waited on the dock. He fell asleep. When he woke up it was to see his mother looking down at him; she looked impossibly chic and beautiful in her black veil and black fur coat. He hugged her, he clung to her like a bear.

152

She said his father wasn't coming until next week. He didn't mind. He'd be the man of the house. He went and hailed a carriage. He put all her bags in front with the driver. He helped her in. She said he'd better ride behind on his bike. He said, no, he'd lock it and ride with her and pick it up tomorrow.

It was a delicious ride through the winter night. He sat under the blanket and clung to her arm all the way. The Victoria clopped around the harbour. Stars glittered above them, the golden light of the carriage's candle lamps flicked along the road, touched the passing shrubs and made happy shadows everywhere it fell.

She was *really* glad to see him. You could tell. She talked and talked and he could smell her special smell, of perfume, of powder and all manner of womanliness. He wished it would go on forever.

He hadn't thought about the Fieldings at all and suddenly they were home and Bill Fielding was beside the carriage.

"I do hope they've been good, Bill," his mother said.

"Oh. We've had our ups and downs," he said. "But nothing serious."

The rat, he squealed later.

The last straw, the last straw. But why had *he* begged . . . ? After all, he'd known, then, that he never wanted to be separated from her again. It must be Fate that's all. That dirty monster Fate.

His watch said almost eleven thirty. It was awful not to sleep, awful.

I might as well get up.

Kling, Kling. Kling, Kling. Kling . . .

The air on deck was bitter cold. Something was different; everything felt heavy, padded. Then he realized he was walking on snow.

Over to the starboard was Halifax but you couldn't see anything. Not a light anywhere. They weren't like Bermuda,

153

they really paid attention to the black-out. He stumbled towards the galley.

"'Ere 'e is," shouted Harry.

"T'is *himself*," Paddy said. "Be Jeesus, it is. Kevin Barrie
come back from the dead."

"Oh. I didn't see you leave the fo'c'sle—I thought you were
still asleep."

"Sleep. Shit. 'Oo wants to sleep. Newsome, ya Geordie sod.
Give the lad a drink."

"Are you daft?" said Newsome. "Shut your bleeding
trap."

"I'll just have some char," said James.

"Come on, Faunty," said Harry, getting up. "I'll show ya
what we got—you can't 'ave any, but I'll show ya."

The place was full of smoke. Harry was staggering. James
knew he must keep very calm. When his uncle was drinking
you always had to be careful not to get him mad.

"Thou art damn fool." Newsome held his cup, on the table,
with both hands. His shoulders were hunched over. "If thou
don't know it's all filthy capitalist trick—"

"Give us some more orange juice."

"Yankee mare's piss, you mean."

Harry led James around behind the counter. "Look-at-
that," he said, bubbling with laughter. "Bloomin' lovely,
in'it?"

At first James thought it was a hot water bottle. Then he
realized that it was for enemas.

"Sh-sh-sh," said Harry, rocking back and forth. "It's pure.
Pure—straight from the sick-bay. Sh-sh-sh."

"Sh-sh-sh your damn self," said Paddy, coming up behind.
"You're a bad drinkin' man, Smith. A noisy one. You'll get
us all in trouble. Here—eat these cloves, you Christly-arse."

"Fuck-off, you old mick brown 'atter you."

"Cloves—for your breath, ya—"

"Shove 'em up your pipe. Let's drink. Look, Faunty." Harry

154

had the tube in his hand. "Just squeeze the titfa—and bob's-your-perishing-uncle." A stream of colourless liquid squirted into his mug. "Muvva's milk."

James got some tea from the urn. It was 11:45.

"Capitalist trick the whole fuckin' war. Use your head. Think. What was Kitchener doing—our best general—*land* man? What was he doing way to fuck up north of Orkneys—on the *sea*, mind? Sea. Land man. It t'were murder. Only one man could stop war. Only one man could lick Kaiser—Kitchener of Khartoum."

"You're daffy, yourself."

"Mind my words. It t'were murder. They pushed him off that ship. T'were a dirty plot."

"Kitchener weren't no good—'e was an *old* man—"

"Thou are damn fools. I've *read* it. T'were a man on cruiser who *saw* Lord Kitchener p*oo*shed—"

"Poosh, yourself. Faunty, 'ave a drink—you miniature H'Anthony Eden, you."

"That's all ancient 'istory."

"Yeh, go and fuck yourself, Newsome."

"Turn-it-up."

"Fuck thee, on my Dad's grave . . . Fuck thee—"

"''Ave you 'eard the one about the blind man on the train to Grimsby—"

"Ancient history, eh? And what about Duke of Kent. That was accident, I suppose? He was only one *on* to 'em—"

"Right up your way too, Newsome. This blind man is on this train, see, and right opposite is this 'ere 'ore—"

"—plane crash, my fanny. He knew too much. And one thing he did know t'were flying."

"—She pulls out one tit and not even *that* gets 'im 'orny. So—"

"Murdered him—just like Kitchener."

"King George wouldn't let 'em, you clot."

"King knows nought—"

"—then she raises 'er skirt and shows her quivering quimm —old hairy-mary itself—"

"—he signs whatever's put in front of him. And what about Hess—now—"

"—no reaction at all—so she shoves 'er finger up 'erself—"

"—disappeared. Murdered he was. Knew too much. And Duke of Hamilton, the young—"

"—right under 'is nose she shoves it. Wipes 'is nose with it. 'Christ,' 'e says, 'Grimsby—' "

"Drink up. *Worse things 'appen at sea.*"

"—they killed him too. A hero, he was. You mark my words, Winston Churchill and—"

"—*Grimsby*, 'ere's where I get off."

"—Adolf Hitler are blood brothers."

Silence.

"—"

"Newsome. You're a fuckin' dripper. Drip, drip, drip all the bleedin' time—"

"Ruin a good party, you would."

"Paddy," whispered James tugging at his arm. "Paddy it's five to twelve—"

"Shut up. Yeh, you boy I mean. Yeh, thee I mean." Newsome's eyes looked vicious. "Thou art jinx—*jinx*!"

"Turn-it-up."

"I mean it. Ship will never get home with him—"

"Fuck-off and leave him be."

"Pad—"

"Lord's bastard."

"Paddy. The bosun will be here *any* minute."

"Jinx!"

"Easy sonny." Paddy's voice was slurred. "Newsome, you're —you know what you are—?"

"Tell 'im, china. Let's 'ave a drink—"

"You're a whore's pelt. A dirty son of a whore's pelt," He

156

spat. "I'd sooner ship with a dozen heathen Chinese than with you—"

Kling, kling. Kling, kling . . .

"Fuck it. Let's 'ave a drink." Harry staggered around the counter. "Cor, wouldn't it be marvellous to just get drunk and stay drunk—forever and ever. *Forever*."

Paddy started singing. "The minstrel boy-oy to the war has gawnnn—in the ranks of dea-eath you will find him—"

"Forever—go on, Paddy-boy, tha's nice."

"His father's sword he hath girded aw-awnn—and his wild harp slung behind him."

"Tha's nice—you singing about Faunty?"

"Faunty?—Faunty?—no, by Jaysus. I was thinking of me-self—"

The black-out curtain opened with a sharp rattle. Chambers stepped in and rattled it shut again. He looked about from man to man. His head tilted forward so that he seemed to look through his heavy eyebrows. "All roight. Who's responsible for this lark? Speak up!"

"Bosun—"

"Shut up, you. We'll start with you, *Smith*."

Harry looked bewildered, like a child whose toy has suddenly been snatched away.

"Well. You're the senior man. What is going on?"

"Easy, Jerry—"

"Don't you Jerry me—I'm not married to ya. Well, what about it?"

"Just a little party like." Harry seemed to be sobering fast. "Don't be a nark, now. We know we're sailing tomorra—"

"Little party. I'll give you little party."

"Well, it's all over now—"

"You're damn right it is. How would you lot like to spend a little time in the chain locker—eh?"

"Come-on, Bosun, be reasonable—"

"*Reasonable*. What 'ave you got? Come on, where is it? I

ought to 'ave you lot up before the First Mate. Let him deal with you."

"Come-on. Not Billings. You wouldn't do that to a—"

"Wouldn't I. Where is it?"

"It was just some gin we 'ad left over."

"Where is it?"

"Gone. Finished it."

"Where's the bleeding bottle?"

"Finished. Over the side."

Chambers moved from man to man, frisking them like a gangster in the movies.

"What are you doing here?" he asked James.

"I'm on watch."

"Well go scrub a pot or something—go on." He turned to Newsome and grabbed him by the shoulder. "Where's Cookie?"

"Take ya hands off me. Think I don't know me rights—"

"I'll give you rights. Where's Cookie?"

"Not here."

"Berkeley. Go find Cookie. Hop to."

James stepped through the curtain and pulled it closed after him.

"—and you lot are bleeding lucky we *are* sailing. Smith, I'm warning you. I've had enough out of you—PAY ATTEN-TION—"

Outside the wind bit at his cheeks. It was like when your hand got stuck, for a moment, against the ice trays at home. This isn't the Atlantic, he thought, it's the stinking Arctic.

If the going gets a bit rough for you down below . . . I could go to the Captain. But Christopher said never give in. Berkeleys don't give in. A gentleman never shows fear. Christopher was fighting the Germans—even if it was in a lousy Lysander—and he'd never give in. Dad was over the side three times and he'd never given in. Teddy had crossed the Atlantic—in worse times than this too—he hadn't given in.

158

God, don't let me give in! But another voice was praying, God give me some excuse to give in. The Captain has two cabins . . .

He could hear his father saying. "What do you mean you couldn't stick it out?—the other men stuck it out. Some Berkeley you are. Some leader!"

"My family are gentry," he remembered his mother had said in a curiously humble tone. "But your father's family— for all their faults—are aristocrats. And don't you forget it!"

Well, he wasn't any aristocrat. He was a lying, stealing, Jew-baiting, over-sexed evil oik juvenile delinquent.

"But I won't give in," he hissed into the darkness. The sound of his own whisper made him shiver. Who said that? Maybe it hadn't been him at all but a ghost . . . some drowned sailor risen from the sea.

VI

Ga-vum, ga-vum, ga-vum, ga-vum.

The convoy, on their port side, seemed to stretch clear around the horizon making a pattern like a fan on the dark grey sea. Grey everywhere save for the splashing white dog-bones at each ship's bow. To starboard nothing but the empty ocean, almost calm now but rising and falling with its monstrous indifference.

Snow was falling, what wind there was was only caused by their forward motion and the sea only rose and fell, James knew, from the disturbance of distant storms and tides. He grasped the rail and watched the snow flakes fall. You could watch one individual flake all the way down; a tiny parachute, a flower and then it touched the water and was gone forever. Every snow flake was different from every other that had ever existed or would ever exist, he knew that. But what difference did it make since their life was so short? Why bother to create them at all?

The sea could swallow up the world—himself.

Ahead of them were five or six ships in a straight line and astern it was the same. The starboard side was a row of sitting ducks, he thought. How safe it would feel if they were in the middle with ships all around them.

But it wasn't the sunny side, was it? And the starboard had been good luck to them before.

Brawnk. Brawnk. Brawnk.

The same as before. Every so often the whole convoy turned like a school of fry chased by a grey snapper. Only at home the fry flashed silver in the transparent sea, flashed and got away.

Flakes of snow eaten by the sea. Eaten up the way the whale, in the encyclopaedia, ate up the plankton and little fishes. The ocean ate up ships . . .

No sun, hardly any day at all and ahead, always ahead, the dark night a minor delirium of long minutes ticked by amid the whirring of engines and the pounding of the screw. Terror endured second by second, minute by minute . . . It had had no beginning within memory; it had no imaginable end. It tore you apart.

Two days out from Halifax the snow stopped but it grew colder and colder. He should put on his long woollen underwear. His mother said to be sure and put on the long underwear. But it looked sissy, they might tease him if they found out: it was enough trouble to try to get the head to yourself for essentials. Besides, it was always so hot in the galley wearing your overcoat and the life-jacket.

"This light goes on automatically when immersed in water . . . " It did too, the men had tried one in a wash basin. What good would it do you, one little light in the whole ocean?

"Wonder if the light would go on if you shoved it up a bit of quimm—eh?"

"Don't be filthy."

"No, it'd be different though, wouldn't it—"

"Red light too—in'it?"

The days nagged by in a monotony of fear. Sleeping, working, eating . . . the alarm bell, when will it go again? But it did not go. It did not go for days.

"If the sea gets up in this cold," said Cookie through his flabby lips, "we'll be for it."

"Aye. Freezin' spray—this fucker's top-heavy enough as it is."

161

"Chroist, we're crawlin. Four, maybe four'n'a 'alf knot—"

"I saw a ship come into Scapa, winter of '38. Cor lummee, looked like a iceberg. No foolin. H.M.S. *Dorsetshire*, it was —but you couldn't tell. Couldn't see nuffin but ice for three days.—"

"Well, that would proper finish this bucket."

"—and them choppin' and choppin' and even thawin' it with steam lines. Three days it took."

"See that escort off the starboard this forenoon?"

"Aye. No fuckin' good. Yankee flood-decker. No Asdic. Yanks don't know a fuckin' thing about Asdic."

"They don't know about fucking nothing. Look at the way this ship is built—it's more like a building, in'it?"

"Yeh. Sea-going skoi-scraper."

"And the lifeboats—bleeding death-traps. No oars—"

"Turn-it-up. Do you expect 'ores at sea?"

"Ha-ha, very funny I-don't-think."

"Better to laugh than drip, in'it?"

"You can say that again."

"What do you do if you can't stop dripping?"

"Last time it 'appened to me I went to a doctor."

"'Ow long before we get 'ome, eh?"

"'Cording to my figurin' ten days." Harry. "Ten days more that is."

"Get stuffed. You don't know what you're talking about. Twenty, I say."

Harry licked his pencil and bent over his notes in the school atlas. "Four days out—well, eleven out of Bermuda. Fourteen outa Balti. Today's the twelfth, in'it?"

"Chroist, and tomorrow's the thirteenth—"

"Don't matter, it ain't Friday though—or is it?"

Harry and Paddy did not pay much attention to him now. When he asked questions they mumbled monosyllabic replies. He decided that it was better to keep quiet for awhile, the way he used to do with his father.

162

Stick-it-out. Don't-give-in. Stick-it-out. Don't-give-in. Stick-it-out . . .

James had just got through the first water-tight door on his way to the engine room when he heard it clang open behind him. He turned. An officer with the girl; he very important-looking, she smiling.

James stood back with the heavy pot in his hands feeling awkward and foolish. Her hair, as yellow as little George's, was gathered back by a blue band. She smiled at James. Her eyes as bright blue as the band.

"Hello," she said.

"Hello," he muttered and looked down at the pot. Just from the way she said hello he knew she wasn't English but Bermudian. From her colouring you could tell she'd spent her life in the sun, swimming and riding and sailing. How had he been so stupid not to notice it before? He wanted to speak to her but he was too ashamed, he felt like a servant.

"I think you'll find this interesting," the officer said and opened the second door. "Noisy but interesting."

She climbed through gathering her skirt, laughing again as if it was all a joke, a picnic. She didn't even have an over-coat and she carried her life-jacket carelessly over one shoulder.

Her legs were very pretty, he thought and everything about her frighteningly feminine. A glimpse of her small sweatered breasts, half-hidden by the life-jacket, but bouncing, softly, roundly as she swung herself through and shook her hair back, gave him a stab of pain deep in his chest.

No comic-book doll this one. No babe to be bound to a chair—God, no. He hurried after them. He wanted to protect her frailty, her littleness; yet he was all too aware that she was inches taller than he was.

Inside the heat and noise only made her laugh. Her laughing,

163

soundless in the din, seemed to ripple on her face and body. Ripple like the warm sun on the water at home.

She can't go down those steps! The men will see up her skirt! But she did. James longed to stop her, to protect her from their eyes. Didn't she know?

Then he imagined himself below. What a joy to look up those legs; maybe she wore little lacey pants, tight around her bottom? A Bermudian bottom like the girls in bathing suits at Coral Beach ... He longed to look up her skirt, her legs; but, conversely, he wanted to protect her from all harm and evil, from the men, even from himself. I would look but I would never tell you.

As she moved down (now reaching to gather her skirt close, now juggling the life-jacket on her shoulder, now looking up for—encouragement? approval?—all the while shaking with silent laughter), that same feminine frailty did something to him that had never happened before: it touched, caught at his groin and left him weak.

She was past the landing now and going down the second flight. He looked below. The men, every overalled oily one of them, were carefully averting their eyes.

Sailors. Jaysus.

He watched, from above, every precious moment, every motion, gesture and intimation ... He feasted on her with a deep and sad happiness.

He tried to carry her memory with him all that day. He lay with her, all unsaddled of life-jackets, warm in a bunk. He would kiss the tip of her nose and her name was Virginia—Veh-ginn-iah—and she was thirsty and he brought her tall glasses of iced-tea with mint-leaves all smokey from the sugar ... and because she loved him he was not afraid and would never give in and he could slay a dragon for her because he was born on the 23rd of April ...

"What ya been doing?" Cookie asked.

164

"Well, we're watching for them Focke-Wolf Condors, doncha know. Tar." The R.N. man, in his yellow-ochre duffle coat, took the mug of tea.

"Never seen one, I haven't."

"Well, I 'ave and we're well over now you know. In their area. Big black baskets they are. Not that they do ya any 'arm —it's 'oo they bring."

James was scrubbing pots.

"'Igh up they stay. Slow moving and then they radio. They direct the subs right to ya. Wolf packs 'n' all. The closer you get to home the worse it is. They'd just like to spot this big convoy too—"

"Can ya shoot them down?" Cookie asked.

"Nar. Never-'eard-of-it. Can't reach 'em—but we can scare them a bit. Christ, when they 'over over you—gives you the wind-up. I've 'ad 'em 'over and 'over, 'ardly moving for hours and hours. Narzi baskets. Mind you, this Orli-gun is a good weapon 'n' all."

"Well, drink your tea, love," Cookie smiled, as always, like a half-baked vicar.

"You after me, you dirty old poofter?"

"'E's 'armless, mate. Don't rile 'im, 'e'll poison the lot of us."

"I don't like the way 'e keeps eyeing that port 'ole."

"No, 'e's too old for port 'ole drill. Aren't cha, Cookie?"

No portholes in the fo'c'sle but portholes here and a porthole in the Captain's cabin and one in Virginia's too. He closed his eyes and tried to see her. But all he could conjure up was a fawn sweater and a blurred flash of skirt and then she was gone . . .

"When I first went to sea, a port 'ole was a port 'ole. You ever got your 'ead out of one they'd close the clamps and . . ."

. . . a wraith whisked away before his mind's eye could rest on her. What would she smell like, his Virginia? Like the inside petals of a rose? You had to be careful not to be seen smelling flowers—it was sissy.

"—God 'elp you."

"On a bad ship, mind—"

"Yeh, Paddy's shark oil 'as been smokey nar for almost two days."

"—your trouziz off and the whole crew would do ya—te-he-he-he." The two-toothed smile.

"Shut up, you dirty sods. What's it mean?"

"Bad weather, you idiot."

"'Asn't it been bad enough? Cold 'n' all?"

"Shark's oil—cor-blimey, what do you take me for?"

"Means a blow, don't it Paddy?"

"Never failed yet, mate."

"Where'd you get it?"

"Show it us, then."

"Havana. A fisherman gave it me—swopped him my knife for it."

"Go on, show 'em, china."

"Bugger 'em. It's in me locker anyway."

"Don't mean nothing."

"Get some seatime in—"

"What should I care what you think—"

"Weather I can't do nothing about—Focke-Wolfs is my line."

"You'd fuck a wolf? Oh you 'owling fucker. You'd *fuck a wolf*?"

"I'd fuck an owl."

"You'd fuck an owl? Oh, you wise fucker. You'd fuck an owl?"

"I'd fuck a chicken."

"Pipe down!"

"You'd fuck a chicken? Oh, you fowl fucker. You'd fuck a chicken?"

"I'd fuck a cheese."

"You'd fuck a cheese? Oh you Krafty fucker—"

"Pipe down. 'Oo do you two think you are—Flannagan and Allen?"

166

"Jaysus."

"Just let 'em come down low—we've the best armed ship in this convoy except for the escorts—"

"You blokes couldn't hit the deck with a bucket a' water."

"Bugger off. You chancred-up—"

"You couldn't 'it a 'ole if you fell in it."

"I could 'it one if it 'ad 'airs around it."

"Turn-it-up."

James made it out on deck and to the rail. The cold air made him feel better and then he found that he was crying which seemed strange because he hadn't had any warning. He wasn't, then suddenly he was.

He reached in his pocket and pulled out one of the silk gloves the R.N. Chief had given him ("Put 'em next to your skin and your regulars on top—keep you warm as toast, lad.") and wiped his eyes.

The alarm bell rang just after noon on the fifth day out of Halifax. The sea was still calm and James got his blankets in the lifeboat without trouble. Sitting in the cold would be the worst part, he thought, but then, no sooner had he thought it than the all clear sounded.

He climbed up in the lifeboat. The sea swished softly below. Again he felt as if he was falling ... He was always falling. McIntyre didn't come aft. He waited and waited and then he threw all the blankets down on the deck. They landed soundlessly. His own bravado made him feel more confident. He climbed down and stowed them away.

Then, again, suddenly he was crying. He wiped his eyes with his gloved hands and tried to spit but his mouth was dry.

How can your mouth be dry and your eyes watering, he wondered? He wiped them again and looked about hoping no one had seen him.

He couldn't see McIntyre anywhere.

"Hey, Faunty. Come 'n' help me with the forward boat."
It was Paddy. "What's up with you?"

"Nothing."

"Eh? What?"

"Bumped my nose on the locker door."

"Smarts, eh? Come on then. Mac has gone sick."

They walked forward.

"What's the matter with Mac?"

"Jaysus, I dunno. Scared, I s'pose."

Paddy climbed up into the boat. He wasn't scared, he was whistling. Just like Chris said, never give in, the other guy will.

"None here" Paddy shouted, "look in the locker."

"They're here."

Paddy climbed down and they walked back along the deck.

"Will you be loading with me now, Paddy—I mean, every-time?"

"Could be. Storm coming though. If it's what I think it's going to be, even Jerry will be too busy to fight."

But the storm didn't come that night nor on the sixth day.

McIntyre had an appendicitis, they said. "Yellowitis," mumbled Newsome and James had to go to the engine room twice as often. He didn't really mind very much because, if his eyes started watering, as they kept doing now so often and without warning, there was less chance of being seen out on deck or moving down the ladders—besides, each time, he hoped he'd see the girl. And then, too, there was something so frightening, so annihilating about descending into this pit that he began, strangely, to welcome it.

James woke up with a nightmare. He felt sick. Almost 11:45 said the luminous dial of his watch. The ship was rolling and pitching, the hull making eerie creaks and groans.

168

Harry was sitting up, pulling his blanket off, rubbing his eyes. "'Ere we go. 'Ere's your dust-up, china and us with the black one again."

On deck the wind whipped his cap off. He grabbed it and shoved it in his pocket and lurched against the deck house. The ship was running downhill, rolling to port and then over to starboard. He staggered around the cargo hatch and made it to the galley.

Cookie put the guards up on the tables and by the end of their watch the cans of dripping, which had begun by slipping quietly and hesitantly across the linoleum, were skidding about like marbles on a tipped bagatelle board. They stowed them in the shelves.

Cookie kept winking at him. James would look down; Cookie was only being friendly, he thought, but he wasn't taking any chances . . .

They lashed the garbage cans to the bulkhead with rope.

"Get's bad, we'll have to do something with them lids. Te-he."

"Is it going to get bad?"

"We had the prop' out of water down from Baltimore— not bad, just noisy."

The ship was running downhill again but the running was halted, stopped by slamming blows like someone punching a sawdust bag . . . then the bow rose . . .

"Be right back," James ducked for the black-out curtain. Outside the wind was vicious now. It wrenched at his coat and almost swept his feet off the deck. He held onto the rail with both hands and took deep breaths. The ship rolled forward again; down, down as if she was never going to come up. Then she shuddered like a wet dog and the bow rose again.

He looked out into the darkness but he couldn't see the ship to port of them. Then he thought he saw the big black shape of a hull up close; a great black wall. He blinked. Now he couldn't see it. Then he saw it again; not a boat, a great giant wave, a wall of sea.

"Berkeley. Get below and turn in," it was Chambers. "Come on. Don't hang about."

Spray ripped over the side, drenched him, stung his face and hands. He started for the fo'c'sle.

"You're not sick, are you?"

"No," James shouted. The wind made noises like spooky movies—only wetter, alive.

"Keep your chin up, lad. Tell Smith I said to watch out for you."

The ship lurched again. James banged into the rail and grabbed hold. Chambers was beside him. "Wait for it." The ship rose up and up. "Now, come on." Chambers pulled him along the deck and through the loop and out to the hatch cover. "Hold it. That's it. Got the idea?"

"Yes." The strong arms let go of him.

"Bugger this for a lark." Harry.

"Turn in, the lot of you. Get some rest. You may need it."

"All right, all right."

"Berkeley. Get in that lower bunk."

"McIntyre's?"

"Yes, McIntyre's."

The ship gave a heavy pound forward followed by a long yaw of the stern. She groaned and pounded again. An electric fan flew off the bulkhead like a cork from a toy gun and banged about hanging from its cord.

"Fucking yankee-built bastard."

"If I ever meet the sod that built this ship—"

Chambers started up the companionway.

"—I'll take out my fanny and piss on 'im."

James climbed up for his blanket. The bananas, hanging from the pipe above his bunk, were banging against the ship's side. He tried to move them further out but felt sick as soon as he touched them. The top ones were green, the bottom ones turning black and messy.

170

Lie down flat, get your head down flat.

He climbed back to McIntyre's bunk. He lay down thinking, vaguely, that he might catch some disease from lying where McIntyre had slept. But that might be a blessing...

He seemed to fight nausea for hours trying to wedge himself...

Then it started. A sudden roaring, a vast vibrating as if the ship was being torn apart. It shook his body so violently that everything he looked at was blurred and jumping. It stopped. The bow rose up and up. His body slipped down until his shoes touched the bunk's bottom rail.

"It's coming right on 'er nose, anyway."

"Wha?"

Then she bucked forward like a bronco—but slow. His stomach seemed to be pushing his chest upwards to his head. Sick rose in his mouth.

G R A H - G R A H - G R A H - G R A H.

The propeller was out of water. He remembered wind-up boats in his bath; if you lifted them their propellers roared like mad too.

It would shake the boat to pieces. They would sink. Why didn't they slow down the engine?

The bow rose again. The noise stopped. Other noises, things clattering to the deck, locker doors flying open...

When he got to the head the noise started again. It shook the bowl he clung to. The whole ship was shaking like a runaway cement mixer. He threw up.

Then, gasping for breath, he felt so much better he thought he was over it. Then he threw up again and the noise came again and then a lurch out of pattern and he missed the bowl.

He pulled himself off the deck, reached the handle and flushed.

God, if the alarm goes now..? The sea. The sea would suck him down... Never give in...

There was a clattering at his feet. It was a bucket rolling about. He thought he ought to do something about the mess.

"Faunty. Get back in your bunk. You hidiot."

"I'm sick."

"Be sick there—not 'ere, you'll get 'urt. Come on."

Back in his bunk he tried to keep himself wedged in again. He'd just get the right position to counter the roll as well as the pitch when it would change.

Clothing, equipment fell from upper bunks. Men cursed. The roaring of the runaway propeller drowned out everything then stopped.

"Fuckin'-arse'oles."

"'Elp me stow this—"

"Shit."

"Forget it—we'll be on deck shortly."

G R A H - G R A H - G R A H - G R A H.

The ship shuddering, screaming in agony.

"Yeh. Chroist it came up fast—"

"Extra look-outs—"

"—Can't keep in convoy long, china."

When he felt sick he leaned out and grabbed the ladder and threw up on the deck. But soon it was mostly the dry-heaves again.

The bosun was shouting something about rigging lines. Then he was sitting on James's bunk holding on to the ladder.

"Stay where you are. If we have to, we'll come for you. *Don't move*. You hear?"

"Yes."

The ship gave gigantic creaks and groans. His watch said past six o'clock. Up on deck there were crashes and bumps and then there was a sound of heavy banging, hammering . . . coming from the head?

The engine was slower now. He could tell by the sound but when the propeller rose out of the water it seemed to roar just as much as before.

172

The convoy. The ship will ram somebody!

The caged lights blinked and blinked again and then went out. He pulled his blanket over his head. He was the only person in the fo'c'sle. They had abandoned him. But Chambers said to stay . . .

Above on deck there was a tremendous crashing and banging. A steam roller had broken loose . . . then he remembered the movie. Humphrey Bogart and a lot of horrible Chinese and torture and a steam roller broke loose and crushed the Chinese and started tearing the boat apart with its gigantic runaway weight. The lights came on again.

He checked the tapes on his life-jacket. Felt the rounded head of the light. He'd go forward until he found somebody, anybody. The men said she'd turn turtle, capsize. He'd be trapped alone.

He got to the top of the companionway but he couldn't open the watertight doors. He was crying again. He looked down to check that the levers were open and then he was thrown outside. Water, a grey blur and he had banged his head and he was on his knees and he grabbed something which turned out to be a big cleat.

"'Ere, Faunty." Hammersmith. "Come on, 'ang on to me."

"I couldn't get out—"

G R A H - G R A H - G R A H - G R A H - G R A H.

"Wha?"

"Out of the fo'c'sle."

"They sent me—hang on."

There were ropes rigged now as extra rails. James put both arms around one. Hammersmith had one hand on James and one on the rope. They were thrown, slurred one way, then the other. Each time James thought the rope would let go and they'd be overboard. But then they were flung back. The ropes seemed like giant elastic bands.

"Easy now. Easy," Hammersmith kept saying. Funny about people, James thought. Hammersmith is brave . . .

173

Water came over the side and drenched them to the skin—gah-voosh, and in the same moment you felt it run down your stomach.

"Hold on chum."

It was like taking a big wave the wrong way at the beach. Grape Bay and the waves over your head. But these waves were over the ship . . .

McIntyre acted tough and is a coward. Hammersmith acted scared . . . maybe Hammersmith was like Destry? But he sure didn't look like Destry. Bullies are cowards, Chris always said. Well, why aren't I a bully then? The Jews . . . I *am* a bully . . .

The ship shook. A wave like a belly punch. She heaved up and over. The rope sagged with their weight. Water poured down.

Buckets of hell . . . Jesus, *God* Himself was a Jew . . .

"Come on, chum."

They made it around to the galley. Hammersmith shoved James towards the door. James slipped, grabbed the door, it swung—Hammersmith's hand! He couldn't stop. Then they were inside.

"My fuckin' fingers."

"Sorry. My fault."

"S'all roight."

"I'm awfully sorry."

"Forget it—s'nuffin'."

Newsome and Cookie were sitting under a table. Crockery and knives and forks and spoons skidded about the deck.

James crawled under the table.

"Hello," said Cookie, "mind your manners—we're having a tea party." He looked at James and laughed. He grabbed his arm. "*Tea party*—didn't you hear?" His eyes looked strange; as if he wanted something but couldn't say what it was. "Tea party." He shook James.

James smiled. Cookie relaxed his grip. "That's it. He-he-he."

"Wish I had a fuckin' drink," said Newsome.

174

James remembered his brandy bottle. He felt for it. It was still there. If he gave it to Newsome Newsome might like him for it. Cowardly. This was no time to trifle with God. Besides, he might need it himself—Dad said . . .

"What do we do if the alarm bell goes?" James asked Hammersmith.

"I dunno."

"It won't—so shudup." Newsome.

"But say we bang into another ship?"

"That's what them poor lads are on deck for—watchin'. Just thank your stars thou aren't them."

After a long silence Cookie grabbed James again. "My garbage broke loose—te-he."

James smiled and pointed towards the counter.

"No. On deck they did. Dumped all over. All dumped. Bosun said don't dump—well Cookie didn't dump—" He shook his head from side to side like Mortimer Snerd.

"Chroist, don't I know," said Hammersmith. "One of them cans chased me across the deck."

"Dumped. All over the Germans . . . He, he, he."

"Yes," said James, "I heard a lot of crashing. I thought the three inch gun had broken loose."

"You can't see nothing out."

"Let's hope somebody can," said James, man-to-man.

"The convoy's scattered by now."

"Chambers 'isself is up the crow's nest."

"A brave man," said Newsome. "If t'would only ease a bit we could get some tea on for the lads."

He was crying again. He felt Cookie's hand on his head. Cookie was stroking his hair.

"Easy. Easy," Cookie cooed.

Taking advantage of a steep roll James moved away.

"What's up?" Hammersmith said.

"Nothing." Never give in. Never . . .

"You're croiin'."

175

"No. Bumped my nose . . . that's all."

"It'll do it everytime," said Newsome.

"Yeh," said Hammersmith, "it'll do it everytime."

James lay in a corner, his feet wedged against one of the legs of a deck-welded chair, his hands holding another. His head rolled about the steel floor feeling like a water-melon in a farm cart.

"Heard no more of him." "Heard no more of him." One of these times they'd just go down and down and never come up. Or else they'd roll over and that would be the end.

If the alarm bell went that would be the end too—he'd be swept, sucked overboard before he could throw the first blanket. Down, down, the fall into the sea . . . the fall and then he'd be swept away, away and astern in the churning swell and then the propeller would be above him . . . Lost at sea. Lost at sea . . .

It amazed him that he could sleep, but he did. He was weak, heavy . . . he seemed to be half-unconscious. He woke, he slept, he woke again.

Men came and went. He stayed where he was. Some kind of watches were arranged. Sometimes soaking wet men came and flopped down near him like exhausted fishes. Sometimes they dragged themselves up again cursing.

Newsome and Hammersmith fired up the stove. He could hear them over the clashing, bumping, over the groans of the ship and gasps of the storm.

The propeller roared, Newsome scalded himself, the loud-speaker said something about a leak in the forward hold and the engine room was calling for Jennings—artificer Jennings. James remembered a waterlogged sign that had washed ashore one day when they were riding the surf. "Keep Out. Engine Room Artificers Only". He had taken the sign home in his bicycle basket and on the way he'd ridden no-handed and

176

eaten a peanut-butter sandwich. It had stuck to the roof of his mouth. Ho-hum, ta-tum . . .

That ship must have been sunk and all the Engine Room Artificers with her . . . Lost at sea, lost at sea . . . The engine room men hardly ever get out.

The convoy had scattered, they said. A Canook corvette had rammed the Commodore, they said. No, no, not *The Reina* and her electric horse and the punching bag. Billings fell down and broke his leg, they said . . . Jack fell down and broke his crown . . . No nursery rhymes please . . . the teasing patterns again . . . Jack fell down—Jack fell down—Jack fell down. Stop. Please stop.

It was fucking night again, they said and a man brought rum. The man was the man who told him to hurry up and get out the day the other Commodore ship got sunk. The quartermaster. No, he didn't want any rum. The smell of it like sick. He had the dry heaves.

Every now and again he started crying and he didn't care . . .

They were drenched with water. A porthole had flown open. Two men were trying to close it; one of them was Harry. Harry. Harry!

Harry was laughing . . .

Chambers had been washed overboard, they said and then Chambers came in and said the forward boat on the port side had been smashed loose and they would have to cut her down.

Water sloshed about, he felt it wet and cold at his groin. He thought he might as well have a pee, he might not get another chance and then he was already doing it.

"Fine fuckin' kettle of fish. I didn't mind when Smith didn't know where we wus—but now I bet the Old Man don't even know."

"'E can't take a sight in this—"

"But it's much calmer like, in'it?"

"Alone again. Luck of this ship—"

177

"But still overcast, you cunt."

"The log—was it carried away?"

"What's it matter. It would make no sense, drift 'n' all."

"Quartermaster'll fix it."

"Alone again—sweet target we are—"

"No. There's a tanker—way off to starboard—"

"And we can make time again without them slow baskets—"

"Don't tell me about no more fuckin' tankers—"

"You can say that again."

"I don't care if I never see another fuckin' sod of a tanker. Jerry will do *any*think to get a tanker."

"Stands-to-reason, don'it. Did you know one tanker can keep the whole R.A.F. flying for nineteen days—"

"I wish we 'ad some nice music. Cor, I'd give anything to 'ear Vera Lynn singin'—just one song." Hammersmith. "One little song—or even Gracie Fields . . ."

"I tell you nobody knows where we are. Not the navigating officer. Not the quartermaster, not the Captain—"

"Well, I figure it's the nineteenth of February—"

"You're just saying that 'cos I said nineteen—"

"No. It's the nineteenth—"

"And the twenty-ninth of February is the Leopard's arse-'ole. 'Ave you 'eard that one?"

"And that's eleven days out of 'Alifax—"

"Go and bugger yourself, Smith."

"And eighteen out of Bermuda."

"Chroist, pipe down, Smith."

"My china can figure you know. He's a proper . . ."

James only knew he had to go to the bathroom. It had been way over four days now. He had just drunk the cocoa Harry brought him and although it made him feel better it had been a mistake because now he needed to go . . . but somehow he *had* to hold it until night. Life was nothing but trying to go and trying not to . . . fear, the sea, toilets, terror were all blurred . . . Time was tearing him apart . . .

Action Stations! Action Stations!
KLAH-KLAH-KLAH-KLAH
Action Stations! Action Stations!
KLAH-KLAH - -
"I told ya—"
"Now, we're *for* it."
"North of Ireland—the worst—"
"Fuckin' night-time. This is it."

His clothes were almost dry again now but they felt very heavy. Everything felt very heavy. The ship seemed to be rolling and pitching almost as much as in the storm. Impossible . . .

This time he barely made it to the companionway ahead of Newsome and Newsome was the slowest man of all . . .

Outside it was very dark. He staggered forward, following the shouts, hoping to find the ladder. The wind was bitter cold. His hat had gone days ago. He didn't know where his gloves were.

He tripped and fell and then he saw a light. A hooded torch. He got up and went towards it.

"Who's that?" The Bosun. "Berkeley?"
"Yes."
"You all right?"
"Yes."
"Get-up-them-stairs, then."

The light shone on the ladder. He grabbed the rail and started up. His body slurred from side to side: utter darkness again. He groped for the second ladder. Then he was crying. He cursed himself and struck at his face.

KLAH-KLAH-KLAH-KLAH

This time we'll get it for sure.

He got to the top of the ladder and then fell again. He crawled on his hands and knees to the port side.

Silence.

Then the sweeshing and swooshing of the ocean below. He

179

clung to the rails. Harry's Oerlikon was below but he couldn't see it.

Swee-eesh. Ga-voosh. Swee-eesh.

The sea was drawing him down again. A horrible magnet. Fate and the sea, they were the same. He clung to the rail.

Peh-tuck. "All passengers, I say again, *all* passengers, regardless of their condition, must assemble in the dining saloon. Stewards will assist—"

"Berkeley. Are those blankets aboard that boat?"

The Bosun. James couldn't talk. He clung to the rail. Blankets? He'd fall with the first one. The sea . . . that little gunwale—he couldn't even see it.

"Berkeley!" Strong arms shook him. "Well then, get below! I've no time to worry about you. Hop to!"

James clung to the rail.

"Get moving. Down to the galley—that's all. Just to the galley."

"I want to go to—to the Captain."

"You balmy?—LAFFERTY—hoi! LAFFERTY."

"Aye!"

"Get up 'ere—boat deck!"

"The Captain said I was—to come to him. He said so."

Chambers was throwing the blankets in the lifeboat.

"Bosun."

"Paddy?"

"Aye."

"Take Berkeley below—then check the boats on the starboard."

"Faunty."

He clung to the rail.

"Jaysus. Come on Faunty or *I'll* cop it."

James got up. He could see a little better now. He followed Paddy down the ladders to the main deck.

"All right, Paddy. I'm all right from here."

"You sure?"

"Yes."

"It's just around the corner."

"Yes."

Paddy went up the ladder.

James knew the way. He'd only been the route twice, once there, once back, but he knew it as if he'd dropped paper like a paper chase or carried a ball of string like the hero of the fairy tale.

He went through the watertight door, along a passage, up some steps, opened another door and stepped through into the light and onto the soft linoleum.

He passed some double doors. DINING SALOON. He heard singing. "Roll Out The Barrel." Raucous and ragged. "We'll have a barrel of fun . . ."

The mat was on the floor. The pale brown curtain, partly drawn, swayed with the motion of the ship. The cabin light was on. He knocked on the door frame. No answer. He looked in. Nobody.

He thought of going in. Maybe he should go in and wait. Not lie on the bed but on the floor. Maybe he could go to the bathroom. It would even have a lock. But the Captain might come and bang on the door. He'd be angry and send him away. Probably back to the fo'c'sle. You couldn't use a man's bathroom without asking.

He started up for the bridge.

"'Ere. Where do you think you're going?" Captain's steward.

James ducked around a corner, saw some steps and ran up them. Some more steps, a cord hanging free, NO ADMITTANCE.

Billings stared right at him. "What? Here, get below. You can't come up here."

The light was strangely dim but James saw the Captain. He dodged Billings. "Come here, boy." Machines ticked. James touched the Captain's arm.

181

"Sir."

"Good Lord. Berkeley, isn't it? Yes. What's the matter?"

"—"

"I'll get him below."

James cringed away from Billings's touch.

"All right, Mr. Billings—Benson. Benson. Take this lad to the sick bay."

"Sick bay's full, sir."

Silence.

Do something. Cry, bawl, anything or they'll send you back . . .

"Well then get him stowed somewhere—my day cabin."

"Sir, Mr. Courtenay-Smith is already there, sir."

James wanted to say that no one was there—he'd just been there. He opened his mouth and tears poured down his face. He was ashamed. Coward. You did it on purpose. Did you? Didn't you? He struck at his eyes with his hands but they wouldn't work properly; they felt like flippers, they wouldn't do what he told them.

"Lord. Well . . ."

His hands were fluttering at the Captain.

"Put him in my night cabin then. Only hurry." The Captain turned. "Quartermaster—"

"Sir."

The cabin was very small. It had a bunk and a desk and a chair. The bunk had drawers under it. The drawers had brass handles on them—Dad.

Benson was looking at him. Benson had a nice face with very pink cheeks.

"You'll be all right?"

James nodded.

"Can't stay I'm afraid. Awfully sorry. Check you later."

He was gone. James looked all around again. A door. He opened it. A lavatory and a basin. The lavatory even had a real seat. He stepped in. A hook for a lock. He hesitated and then pushed the hook over.

He took down his trousers and sat on the seat. It was heaven. Then he burst into loud sobbing tears.

VII

When James woke up he saw the Captain sitting at his desk. The Captain's head was down cradled in his arms, he was quite still.

The ship seemed still too, still and almost silent. Then he could hear the engine pounding softly and the vents humming —everything had a padded, cushioned sound up here. Luxury. But the ship wasn't rolling . . .

Something was wrong. Then he remembered: he had gone to sleep on the floor and now he was in the Captain's bunk. The Captain must have lifted him there. He had gone to sleep on the floor because he thought the Captain . . . He had taken one blanket and lain down on the floor. It was just after he had gone to the bathroom. He remembered, he'd sat on the lavatory and when he'd finished he had smelled his trousers to make sure they didn't smell of pee because he remembered that in the storm he'd . . . and they didn't smell of anything but the ship: oil, paint and a little garbage. But he'd thought he was too dirty to get in the bunk—the Captain's bunk.

The ship hummed along like a train. She wasn't rolling at all. Why? Where were they?

Then the Captain moved, groaned slightly and was still again.

The storm, the alarm, the sea . . . I'm safe. Safe for a while from the fo'c'sle, the galley, the lifeboat, the fall into the sea . . .

Kling, kling. Kling, kling . . .

Seven bells. Seven-thirty his watch said.

He heard steps going by in the corridor. People laughing. A few words and then the steps receded. The only word he'd heard was gurr-ruk and he didn't know what it was. Virginia laughing . . . Dad. I quit. I gave in. I am a coward. I am no longer worthy to be called your son.

He thought he'd better try to get to the Captain's head for a pee before the Captain woke up.

Christopher, I quit—I gave in.

His shoes touched the linoleum with only the slightest of sounds. The Captain's head popped up like a horse startled in its stall.

"Yes, what is it?" he said, looking at the door. "Come— oh, it's you, Berkeley."

"Yessir. I'm sorry I woke you up. Sorry I took your bunk—"

"Forget it boy. How do you feel now?"

"Much better, thank you, sir."

"Good, good. Well, look out of the porthole."

James hesitated. Porthole? Surely not the Captain . . ?

"Go on. Look out. There's a surprise for you. Better than any tonic."

James stood up. As soon as he turned he saw it—green where grey had been, land. A green rounded hill. Land—soil, earth. He ran to the porthole.

Dark-grey calm water and grey sky, but land. Sweet rounded green hills with grass right down to the water's edge. And houses, *real* houses nestled along the shore, nestled into the hills—and people were in them. Real people, you could tell, because smoke, real blue whispy smoke came from the funny-looking little chimney pots.

"Where are we, sir?"

"The mouth of the Clyde, boy. That's bonnie Scotland."

"I can see a town, sir."

"That'll be Gren-nock or Gurr-ruk."

Crazy names, he thought and then he realized he was crying again.

Brur-urp.

The Captain picked up the phone.

James went into the bathroom and hooked the door. He blew his nose hard on toilet paper, had a pee, washed his hands and then looked at his eyes in the mirror. He blew his nose again.

He ought to be happy, he thought and he was happy—but something was all wrong. It was raining on his birthday, there was no doubt about that. Life felt like one lousy drizzly rainy day.

One lousy night. If I'd just stuck it out . . .

"Well, don't look so miserable. You need a good wash 'n' brush-up, boy." The Captain smiled. "You can take off that damn thing." He pointed at the life-jacket.

James undid it. "Will I be able to go ashore, sir—I mean today?"

"Don't see why not." The Captain pushed a bell button. "Where are you bound—south?"

"To London, sir."

"Well, you can take the train to Glasgow and change there —have you got enough money?"

"Yes sir. Ten pounds my father gave me."

"That'll be plenty." The Captain drummed his fingers on the desk.

"I've never changed trains before, sir. Could you tell me how to do it?"

"What? Well, I'd better send someone along to put you on the London train. How about that?"

"Thank you very much, sir."

"Anyone in particular you'd like."

"Well I'm friends, sort of . . . with Harry Smith and Paddy Lafferty—"

186

"Can't have both, you know. Who shall it be?"

"Smith, please sir."

"Right you are. Well—"

The steward popped his head in. "Sir?"

"Get Berkeley's belongings from below, will you, and take 'em to my cabin."

"Yessir." The steward disappeared.

"Give my apologies to Mr. Courtenay-Smith, Berkeley, and tell him I sent you—all right."

"Yes sir."

"You have yourself a good wash—a shower, change your clothes. Right? Right then, run along."

"Sir?"

"What is it?"

"Thank you . . . thank you for the trip, sir. I had a very nice time."

"What?" The Captain smiled. "Yers—well, quite—run along, there's-a good lad."

The steward brought up his things, even the bananas. Mr. Courtenay-Smith took his silver penknife and cut off the dead ones.

"Steward, clean these shoes, will you. And could you press these trousers?"

James stood in his underwear.

"Them?" said the steward pointing at James's trousers. "Couldn't do nothing with them, sir."

"Do you have any others?"

"Only in my trunk, sir."

"Trunks is going ashore now, sir."

"Well, brush 'em up a bit, steward—and see what you can do with this overcoat."

"Coo, sir, I'll try."

In the bathroom James carefully took five pounds from his chamois pouch and put them in the wallet he had

187

bought, so long ago, with the stolen money. He still felt dizzy.

In the shower he rolled from side to side. The ship was still but he kept rolling. The sea still seemed to be washing, pouring over everything.

He got dressed, carefully knotting his tie and fastening the tie pin the way his father did. Then he went aft and stood by the rail looking down over the lower deck. The sun was out over the deep green hills, it was pale but it was out.

The hatch-covers were off and some men were unloading luggage into a tender. In the very first load he saw hauled up was his trunk; a squashed-looking leather one covered in out-dated labels. Not Wanted On Voyage, he remembered reading ... Mother's bedroom ... he had wondered, vaguely, what it meant. The whole load was pulled up by one of the crane arms attached to the main-mast. He looked up. The mast was still against the sky, the look-out platform empty.

He looked down again.

He didn't recognize any of the men. He thought he should go down and say goodbye to the seamen in the fo'c'sle but he was ashamed. Then he saw Newsome leaning against the gun-wale looking at the northern shore. The shadow of the crane-arm passed across him; he moved, looked up and then spat over the rail.

James went back to the Captain's cabin. Mr. Courtenay-Smith wasn't there and all his things were gone.

Harry knocked at the door. He was wearing a leather jacket and a pair of American khaki trousers and his hair was slicked down.

"Well, are you ready then?"

"Yes. Do we go ashore now?"

"Aye."

"I hope this isn't too much trouble, Harry?"

"Na. Nothing-at-all."

188

"Turn-it-up, darling. Just lemonade."

"All right. All right. Oh, look, bananas, fancy that."

James smiled.

"Only make mine black 'n' tan, love."

"Make up your mind."

"Black 'n' tan and a side order of tricksey."

"Regulars only, sailor. But you can have the lemonade and black 'n' tan."

"Come-off-it. I'm no sailor, I'm with the Secret Service. Give us a drop—"

"Nothing doing."

"A dram then, you lovely lassie."

"Is there anything else you'd like, your lordship?"

"Yeh. I'd like to walk with you beside the bonnie banks of the Clyde. Lordship!? Nark-it. This 'ere is 'is Lordship."

"Where are you from, Australia?"

"Dangerous Talk Costs Lives, lass, don't it? But truthfully I'll tell ya. I'm fresh in this morning from New York see. In a flyin'-boat. Special orders from Winston Churchill. This 'ere nipper is Mr. Roos-a-felt's nephew—on 'is mother's side, that is. 'E's been sent over for the duration—for safe keeping. You know, away from the bombing."

"Yes, yes."

"It's terrible the way those Japanese are bombing America. Nar, give us a whisky, love, and later we can take a walk, eh? When do you get off?"

"You better watch it. My husband would tear you apart."

"Yeh, and most likely 'e's in Cairo. Besides, maybe you've 'eard of me. Farr. Tommy Farr?"

"No fooling. I took you for the Duke of Windsor. That'll be one 'n' sevenpence sailor, and watch your lip."

Harry paid her and then leaned across the bar. "Now, darling, listen. I'm putting the nipper on the train in a little while—to London. Then I'll be back for ya—roight?"

"I don't have nothing to do with common sailors."

"Come-off-it. I'm rich too. Three months pay—"

"Lot of good that'll do me—"

"You can say that again; but slow—lot-of-good-that-will-do-me."

Harry had another pint and went on talking to the barmaid. James went and found the men's room. It was just black slates up against a wall with a trough at the bottom but it was the place: he could smell it and the slates were stained yellow and white.

Life, he thought, is full of toilets—each one more disgusting than the next.

He tried to pee but heard someone coming and it wouldn't work. But no one came in and finally it worked.

Then he carefully undid his shirt, reached in and got another pound from his chamois pouch. He'd give it to Harry; Harry would like that. Harry was his friend; they were chinas.

At the station a woman porter tried to take the trunk.

"Get-out-of-it," said Harry.

They put the trunk in the luggage compartment and then Harry found him a corner seat. The train rapidly filled up with passengers; mostly men and women in uniform.

"Well, I gotta be off Faunty boy."

"Here, Harry. This is for you. And thank you so much—for everything."

"Come-off-it! What do you take me for?"

"No, no. My father said—"

"Tell you what. You could pay me back for the lemonades—it was two, wasn't it? Eightpence."

"But I owe you for the sausage rolls and everything."

"Don't insult me now—just eightpence."

James fumbled in his pocket and found a shilling. Harry carefully counted out four pennies and handed them back.

"And you could give us a few bananas if you like."

"I can't. They're not mine . . ."

192

"Forget it then."

Silence.

"Well, so long, Faunty."

"—"

And then the train was moving. Now he felt homesick for the bar . . . The world was still rolling and pitching, the sea still washed over everything.

M'mum. M'mum. M'mum.

He took the label out of his pocket. His father's neat printing. JAMES BERKELEY. DELIVER TO: JOHN SOMERS ESQ, 12 BISHOPSGATE, LONDON E.C.2.

Be fucked if I'll wear that poofter thing.

But then he was crying again. He turned his head away and pretended to be looking out of the window. Now the rails were saying:

Lost-at-sea, lost-at-sea . . . heard no . . . heard no more . . . no more of him, no more of him, no more . . .

Words Left Over After Writing About War

The year before my voice
broke
our convoy left Halifax
with over forty ships
and reached Greenock with
nineteen.
No heroics
just grey white-flecked
ocean
and sky
and sometimes the spray was frozen when it
hit the deck.
There were bumps in the night
and I seemed to live in the latrines
and once, on a bright day,
I leaned over the rail
and watched our ship
plough through
and down
the bobbing heads
of the seamen
torpedoed on station in front of us.
One head, in memory,
seems to rise higher
than the others:
it has bruised and blackened
eyes
and shouts in anger, fury,
beating the waves
like a turtle,
"save ME!"

The voice is now my own.